Once a Guyanese Child

– Zorina Ishmail-Bibby –

ONCE A GUYANESE CHILD
Copyright © Zornia Ishmail-Bibby 2009

All rights reserved.

No part of this book may be reproduced in any form by photocopying or any electronic or mechanical means, including information storage or retrieval systems, without permission in writing from both the copyright owner and the publisher of the book.

ISBN 978-184426-552-7

First published 2009 by
FASTPRINT PUBLISHING
Peterborough, England.

Printed by
www.printondemand-worldwide.com

Information about two of the charities which will receive donations from the sale of this book.

MOPSA

(Missionaries of the Poor Supporters' Association)
Registered Charity No. 1048926

There are many homeless and destitute people throughout the world, but especially in third world countries. The Missionaries of the Poor is a religious congregation which runs residential centres for the poorest of the poor in Kingston, Jamaica, in the Philippines, in India, Haiti, Uganda and Kenya.

There are more than five hundred who give free service to the poor, not only in the centres, but also through the distribution of food to many others in slum areas. The homeless, those suffering from Aids, orphans, and the mentally or physically disabled of all ages are helped.

MoPSA exists to raise money for the Poor, and nothing is kept aside for overheads, which are donated separately. Some of the members of MoPSA have visited and worked in the centres in Jamaica and know personally many of the brothers, including the founder and superior, Father Richard Ho Lung. This personal knowledge of and interest in the recipients of our gifts enables us to give with confidence and generosity.

I am most grateful to Zorina for offering to donate some of the proceeds from the sale of this most interesting and inspiring little book to the work of MoPSA.

Chairman of MoPSA
Father Ken Payne.
St Aidan's Church

Sightsavers International

Sightsavers works in over thirty countries worldwide. Their activities follow three key principles:

1. Working in partnership with those who implement projects. These may include health and education ministries or community based organisations.
2. Influencing policies which help people who are blind or visually impaired.
3. Joining to work with organisations e.g. The World Health Organisation which aims to eliminate avoidable blindness by 2020 and prevent 100 million people from going blind.

They also try to provide solutions to prevent :
- River blindness.
- The spread of Trachoma.
- Distribute Mectizan in order to prevent childhood blindness.
- Work with communities worldwide in health and care.
- Train local health workers to deal with basic eye care so they can work in their own communities.

For more information, go to www.sightsavers.com

Other Charities

Some other charities Zorina hopes to donate to after expenses are covered:
- Northampton Association for the Blind
- Cynthia Spencer Hospice, Kettering Road, Northampton.
- Cats' Protection League

Introduction

I came from a culture of storytelling. My maternal grandmother was a country woman. She knew much about healing, herbs, folklore and Nansi stories.

Although Grandma had been removed from school very early in life, she was a shrewd business lady. I think this skill came from having to take care of her blind mother (a very assertive lady) and two young sisters. She had to run the house on a tiny budget. Grandma could not read but had inherited a passion for storytelling from her mother. So as a child, whether it was on the veranda, in the house or kitchen, I was treated to stories.

This collection of short stories started when I first finished college in the U.K. I was refused work as a teacher in my area of the Corentyne in Guyana. There was a dire need for teachers but the political situation of that time was not favourable.

These stories followed soon after the refusal. I first wrote "In Gramma's Kitchen", then others came to me over the next few years. They were conjured up and set in Guyana but followed me around to St. Andrews, my first real home in the U.K. and then back to the Midlands.

Long before "Multi-culturalism" became a buzz word in education, it prevailed in 79 village in the Skeldon area of the Corentyne River, Guyana. Here I spent my earliest years of childhood. The plantation system of Guyana had thrown Amerindians (Arawaks and other indigenous people), Africans, Indians, Portuguese, Chinese, Scottish, English and people of other cultures together.

As a small child in my area, there was a real sense of community. But there were outsiders like the sad Onion and Garlic in my short story.

Later with political changes, the struggle for power, imposed shortages of food and materials, life changed. Many people emigrated to the west. Guyana was a British colony where the county of Demerara had produced rich brown sugar for over a hundred years. It was the only British colony in South America.

Although I lost my homeland, these stories, unconsciously became vehicles of the imagination for travelling back in time. Photographs of my family and friends are included to give a flavour of the period when the main character, Zohra, was growing up. It was a world new, exciting but full of surprises and lessons, helping Zohra to learn about life's chequered pathway.

I am extremely fortunate for I gained a second home in the U.K. Dear friends, like Betty Burn, offered me respite when I was a young student and I still return to Kirkcudbright, Scotland to visit her. She also introduced me to Ann Karkalas from Glasgow University when I first began writing these short stories. Ann became a friend who always offered constructive criticism and support over the years.

My first real home was in St. Andrews, Scotland and when I settled there, the stories for this collection came thick and fast. I worked part time at the St. Andrews University library. When I had time off, I was fortunate enough to help set up Hope Park Playgroup with empathetic friends like Dr. Sheila

Lenman and Wendy Quinault. My time in the playgroup and with a Creative Arts Workshop for children must have contributed to understanding how children functioned. I enjoyed it enormously.

Over the years good friends like Ian Lakin and his mother, Florence, the Harrisons from the Midlands have made me feel very at home in the U.K.

In the 1980's I was Chairperson of the then NATESLA (National Association of Teachers of English as a Second Language to Adults). I feel my multicultural background contributed to helping us change our title to NATECLA (National Association for Teaching English and Other Community Languages to Adults).

As County Coordinator for English to Speakers of Other Languages in the late 1980's and 1990's, I could identify with different cultures and the needs of displaced and traumatised refugees.

Sadly, my grandmother, aunt and mother are no longer with us and cannot read this collection of short stories. I hope they would have enjoyed them. My mother was a great reader and insisted that I read Dickens when I was about eight or so. Now I am amazed I did, but thank you, Mommy!

I must thank Debjani Chatterjee who edited Mango Shake (published by Tindal St Press Ltd. 2006) and selected Ole Man and Miss Gusta's Lil' School for her collection of short stories. She has been a friend, poet and writer for many years. She has encouraged me to publish both prose and poetry when I was unsure about what route to take.

Missionaries have had a bad press in the past. . I am sure this may have been justified. Yet in areas of Guyana like the Corentyne, we would have had no education in the 20th century if Christian missionary organisations had not set them up. There were Catholic, Anglican, Lutheran, Scottish, Presbyterian and other schools which helped educate us. This is reflected in my stories.

I also thank Father Ken Payne and Father Hu Long for all the work they do for the M.O.P.S.A. I hope after recovering my publishing costs for this book to donate any profits to M.O.P.S.A. and Sightsavers International and other charities if this collection makes enough funds. M.O.P.S.A. supports homeless, displaced and poor people in Jamaica and other parts of the world. Sightsavers works to help the blind and those with poor sight in third world countries.

Some of these short stories have been published in the past or broadcast on the World Service. However, the whole collection has never been published in continuity showing the child's growth and development.

I would also like to say thanks to Lesley Nuttall, a friend and former secretary in Adult Education for word processing this collection. As a grandmother, she has kindly appreciated Zohra's adventures – I think!

Zorina Ishmail-Bibby. 2009

This book is dedicated to Grandma, Aunty and Mommy who shaped my life as a child and gave me the basics to survive away from my homeland.

Three Women

I remember my mother
Resting after lunch
As I tiptoed into the room
Jalousied from sun.
Her bangles flashed gold
Kiskadees, fluttered along
Brown skin, reaching
For the fan on her bed.
I remember coolness
Of my aunt's flesh,
Hollowed by my cheek
On hot nights when moon
Panted breathless on water
And the vast sky bowed
Down to meet the earth.
I remember Grandma's tilary
Splendouring from her neck
Worn at births, funerals, deaths.
"No chile," she'd say. "Don't touch.
Did it ask to be touched?"
It did. Gold spoke, whirled me
Into strange patterns,
Then filigreed me out again.
And I lived wound in gold
Of three women's selves,
Thread of their fabric,
Listening for the sky's fall
And the land's rise.

Zorina Ishmail-Bibby
From *"After a Cold Season – Rising"*

*This collection is also for my brother,
Sid and sister, Fadia who grew up while
I was abroad, and Kem, my other brother,
who moved on.*

Corentyne Days

Houses were fat prima donnas
Balancing on slim stilts, sunwhite.
Eaves and jalousies, wooden lace,
Filigreed and gauzed Sundays
When churchbells rang awaking
Cousins cuddled in brass beds
Still enmeshed in tales of last night.
The Ole Hags flew high
In roofs bungalowed,
Downturned storybooks,
Hiding and seeking out
Our fears among rafters,
Spellbinding us with dreams
Until daybreak and release.
Days were packed with play
Ferryspotting, marble pitching
Mango raiding, gorged on flesh
Ripe as our young lives,
Arms golden with juice,
Mouths purpled with jamoons
We rivalled our rain forest
Kin, greedy and wild.
Then river washed, human
Again at moonrise, Nansi
Stories flowed on verandahs
Frangipanied and oleandered
With scent, till intoxicated,
We yielded to fantasy.
Yet unaware all the while
Our minds turned on the lathe

> Of imagination storing
> Images for comfort to warm us,
> Adults in cold places, exiled
> Far from home in times hard
> As bunga seeds in dry season.

Zorina Ishmail-Bibby
From "*Her Mind's Eye*"

A Corentyne Village

Contents

1.	The Child, The House And The Cinema	5
2.	In Gramma's Kitchen	13
3.	Miss Gusta's Lil' School	26
4.	The Threat	37
5.	A Kite Like Christ	45
6.	Pigeon Stew	58
7.	Onion And Garlic	66
8.	The Masqueraders	77
9.	Cheat	95
10.	The Move	103
11.	Ole Man	115
12.	Reconciliation	123

Cover Details

The front cover painting by Zorina has been inspired by memories of the Corentyne coast in Guyana and other images of tropical beaches all over the world

Photographs in this book

All photographs are from Zorina's collection of family photographs. The photograph inserted in the painting on the front cover was taken and designed by Kamal Ishmail, photographer, in the 1980s.

The front cover painting and design has been done by Zorina.

Once a Guyanese Child

– Zorina Ishmail-Bibby –

Once a Guyanese Child

Child on Wooden Horse

Once a Guyanese Child

1. The Child, The House And The Cinema

Some of Zohra's earliest memories were of Capa's house and cinema. She had always called her grandfather 'Capa' as long as she could remember. He had built the house and cinema. Zohra loved them because they belonged to him. Now Capa was dead and as she wandered around looking for him she only found his house and cinema. Somehow they made her feel safe for they seemed too large and solid to disappear as Capa had done.

Capa's house came alive when the afternoon heat reduced the village to siesta and sun glinted metallic on vegetation. Then the house sprawled like an overgrown youth and its shingled walls blushed pink.

"Capa house like overseer from the canefield when they walk in the sun," Zohra used to think, remembering an Englishman she once saw in the cane fields.

Though the outside of the house seemed young to Zohra, the inside felt immeasurably old. Maybe the sweetness of the decaying crabwood gave it the feeling of age. Zohra did not know. But she liked the combination of youth and age. It harmonised as she had done with Capa. She felt safe.

Upstairs, darkness stayed in the corners and evaded sunlight. There was a dark corner at the bottom of the enclosed staircase which led down to the bathroom and kitchen. Shadows haunted this place. It fascinated the child and each day she tested her courage at Azan time when darkness thickened and daylight disappeared.

Everyday at six o'clock, Azan, the call to prayer, echoed through the village. Other children had told Zohra that at that time Jumbees and Ole Hags began to stir in their sleep at the burial ground. They said later in the night these evil beings came to steal Man's soul and drink his blood.

Zohra remembered Roseta whom the other children called Ole Hag. This woman stood for hours staring into the water by the Koker. Sometimes, after school, the children would run past yelling:

"Hey Ole Hag! What you come out now for? It ain't night time yet!"

She answered with threats and curses which only silenced the children temporarily. They were convinced she was an ole hag and drew chalk circles to entrap her, but Roseta was too clever. She always escaped them. So she remained an object of taunts, stones and chalk circles. This was how Zohra came to associate her with Jumbees and evil.

The cinema, Metro, was also an important place for the child. Sometimes, she spent her afternoons there with Henry, the caretaker. He was a special friend for he allowed her to wander freely around the cinema. Whenever Zohra could, she slipped away from the house and went to Metro though her mother disapproved. But Zohra's eagerness to visit Henry only increased in this atmosphere.

One day, she took her doll in the pram and wheeled it past the vat of water in their backyard. Grandma's chickens squawked and scattered before her charge. Grip, the dog, followed, occasionally stopping to scratch away his fleas. They went up the red brick track to the cinema and stopped before it. Metro's panelled shutters were plastered with posters. Zohra turned to Grip.

"Now Grip, if you ain't good, Henry won't let us near the film stars."

Zohra believed the film stars lived behind the screen. Henry had not rejected this idea. Zohra felt Henry was a very important person. He lived backstage near the film stars and some of their glamour had rubbed off on him. Besides, she

Metro Cinema

liked the hollows in Henry's cheeks and his black moustache which he let her touch occasionally.

At this time, Zohra failed to see his loneliness. He had no relations. No one cared whether Henry sat watching till cockcrow, but Zohra loved him. Through the stifling walls of night, his hollow cough would ring, comforting her during nightmares and stretches of sleeplessness. Then awareness of Henry's presence outside, would lull her back to sleep.

Now however, Zohra only wanted to enter the cinema. She took her doll Pam in the pram up the path. At the entrance, loud posters, heralds of coming films, plastered on the front of the building enticed her in. She grew excited as she looked through an open shutter.

"Henry, we all come to help you sweep."

Sybil-like, her voice echoed in the cinema's cigarette smoke. Henry, lost in an infinity of cinema seats, looked up. His cigarette quivered comet red.

"Come sit in balcony and see how me sweepin'."

"No, me and Grip come to help you sweep."

"You Mommy go vex if you dirty yourself up."

"Me got to sweep, else me won't be near the stars."

Her tearful voice prompted Henry to give her a pointer broom, made from the ribs of coconut fronds. Though it was the same height as Zohra, she eagerly wielded it, creating a miniature dust storm, of which she became the centre.

The child swept her way to the stage where the screen towered. Then triumphantly climbed the platform and peered through. Zohra saw grey shadows within. Excitedly, she identified them – bad witch from 'Hansel and Gretel' and the countess from 'The Three Musketeers'.

"Come down or you go fall!"

The characters shrivelled again into shadows as Henry spoke.

"But me watchin' the witch. Now you make she disappear!"

"You know you Mommy won't send you back if you fall down,"

"Me didn't fall down."

"Come down like a good gal, and me will give you toffee."

The temptation of toffees rated only secondary to watching the stars. After much coaxing, she eventually agreed to leave the stage. It cost Henry six toffees, three bits of cigarette paper and his promise to let her see the film 'Macbeth'. So Zohra exchanged her high place on the stage for the low one in the wasteland of cinema seats.

She hugged Pam, placed her feet on Grip's back and twisted her head to catch glimpses of spectral film stars.

"The screen look small from here. How they can fit in? Where they put their car?" she asked. "You know anythin' 'bout it, Henry?"

"Eh, heh," Henry said.

The sucking of toffee stopped; there was a sigh, then a gasp.

"Why I so stupid? Film stars magical! It so easy. All they gotta do is wish. Then they can get big garages to put them in."

Zohra's imagination bewildered Henry. But he never let it spoil their friendship. He humoured her by making non-committal sounds while she talked to herself. So they were happy together.

"Why me can't get inside the screen to become a film star, eh Henry? Then you can wish for you to come live with me."

"Uh-huh."

"Me know what. Me is the witch from 'Hansel and Gretel'!" she shrieked, jumping up, much to Grip's discomfort and Henry's alarm. Her voice resounded sharply in the cinema.

"Don't keep so much noise, gal! You want to send me deaf?"

"No. I just playin' the witch."

"But you don't see you disturbin' the film stars, man."
"What?"
"Shh. They sleepin'."
"Oh, yes. They sleepin' after they work so hard by night."

Henry continued to sweep in peace. But Zohra never wondered why the constant swish of his broom did not wake the film stars. She just sat hugging Pam and thinking about them.

"Zohra, you better go for breakfast," Henry said.
"What, is time?"
"Yes. Is twelve o'clock and you Mommy will worry 'bout you."

Zohra rose and walked from the safe darkness of the cinema into the hole in the shutters which led to the outer world of blinding sunlight.

"Don't forget 'bout 'Macbeth', Henry. We make a bargain."
"O.K. Is a bargain. Come at four-thirty p.m. sharp Wednesday afternoon."

The poster boards by Metro cinema had first attracted Zohra. It read 'Macbeth' which baffled her. The name 'Macbeth' seemed strange. But the incongruity between the men's unkempt beards and frock-like clothes puzzled her even more.

"Mommy, what 'Macbeth' mean?"
"Is the name of a bad king Shakespeare write 'bout. You remember 'Hamlet'? He write that play too."
"The one with the ghost?"
"Yes."
"And why they dress like lady?"
"So people dress in those days."
"Me goin' to see it 'cause it look so funny,"
"You did frighten last time when you see 'Hamlet'. You can't go this time."
"But I gotta go, Mommy."

"No."

Zohra did not argue anymore. She waited for Wednesday to come and slipped away to see the film that afternoon.

"They talkin' so strange," Zohra thought. "But is a good story so far. Them witches like Roseta and the Ole Hags who fly about at night time. But the film stars will tie them up inside the cinema. They won't get out to suck us. Anyway they gone now."

Macbeth went back to his castle and Zohra felt safer. She began to enjoy the film.

"Them swords so sharp and them men in short dress look like thiefman. And Macbeth wife like Kalamadin wife next door. They like to quarrel."

But when Macbeth entered the witches' cave, Zohra's palms began to sweat. The witches chanted as they threw toads, lizards' legs and dogs' tongues into the cauldron. They spoke so slowly and clearly that even Zohra could not miss the words. She trembled, for she could remember contented toads sitting by the vat, and she had seen lizards flash by, full of life.

"And they hurtin' nice puppies like Grip. How he can bark without his tongue?" she thought terrified.

The shapes of people around her became ominous. They were spirits conjured up by the witches. The darkness of the cinema she loved grew menacing. She thought the witches had called up Capa from the burial ground and he would appear to her at any time. Zohra slid to her knees behind the seat and peeped at the screen between the chinks of the seats. The Weird Sisters had changed everything. Roseta became a symbol of living evil and Zohra was now truly afraid of Jumbees and the dark.

"They kill the film stars and come out from behind the screen," she thought, yet she could not stop looking at the film.

"Macbeth" ended. The rest of the audience left, but Zohra sat on till Henry discovered her.

"Is time to go home, Zohra."

Zohra's fear burst out with a flood of words.

"The witches loosing Capa from burial ground at night time!" she cried. "They and Roseta will kill us – and Grip too!"

She clung to Henry.

"Is only pictures, Zohra."

"No, is real. The Jumbees and Ole Hags livin' behind the screen. The film star gone."

Gently, Henry led her outside. She stayed close to him, even though she recognised the familiar silhouette of Capa's house and the throb of the electric generator.

"They still here, Henry." She kept saying.

"Nobody there but us, chile."

But Zohra could not accept this. To her, the night seemed endless and as long as there was darkness the Ole Hags and Jumbees would stay.

2. In Gramma's Kitchen

Gramma's kitchen was another important place in Zohra's life. After a while, the stove, the fireside, trunk and traff became well known areas in Gramma's kingdom.

These objects had existed as long as Zohra could remember. The stove had always devoured wood and spat out orange flames. Next to it, the window overlooking the soursap trees sometimes framed fiery sunsets. Then the fire in the stove resembled these sunsets but outlived them for hours after they had died away,

Unlike the stove, the fireside scared Zohra when she was smaller.

"Gramma, Zohra don't like fireside," she persisted, retiring to the trunk by the trough.

"Why?" Gramma asked, but Zohra could not explain.

The fireside reminded the child of the unmarked graves in the village cemetery. Dimly, she remembered a maid once taking her past the burial ground. Zohra misbehaved and the woman had threatened to leave her to the Jumbees in those graves. So Zohra grew up fearing the fireside except when the fire blazed within it.

"All the Jumbees goin' to burn up if fire light," Zohra thought.

Zohra liked the trunk. Gramma used it mainly as a cupboard for storing flour, rice, sugar and saltfish so the mice could not reach them. Years of scrubbing had turned the wood white and Gramma rolled dough for roti on the top. Zohra sometimes rubbed her nose against it.

"Why you doin' that?" her Grandmother would ask.

"It smell like roti crumbs here," Zohra replied.

"What you go think of next?" her Gramma would say shaking her head in wonder.

The trough, or traff on the other hand, made Zohra yearn to grow older. Traffs were primitive wooden sinks used for dish-washing and usually fixed outside the kitchen window. More fortunate people had water pipes attached to theirs; others had to take heavy buckets of water from outside into the house to wash their dishes. Capa's house was very old. The traff had no pipe. So Gramma fetched water from the vat in the garden upstairs to the traff.

Once Zohra was allowed to help Gramma. But she spilt so much water on the stairs on Gramma's skirts that she was no longer allowed to so do. Now Zohra walked behind Gramma, and imitated her as she carried her bucket. The child would lean to one side and hold up her dress the way Gramma did. Her cousin Amin had teased her about this once.

"Why you always follow Gramma when she carry water, eh? You look so stupid."

"Gramma don't mind. Anyway you play cake shop like Uncle Mus. I don't laugh at you then."

As Zohra grew, these four areas of curiosity acted as touchstones for other experiences. They helped to translate her relationship with strangers she met in the kitchen. In this way, Gramma's domain extended from the stove, fireside, trunk and traff to visitors. Zohra had always been aware of shadowy figures coming to visit Gramma. Yet they remained remote, half-forgotten dreams until the day one dawned on her.

A heavy voice spoke. It filled the kitchen, reverberated from the hollow unused fireside, bounced against the stove and trunk, then disappeared by the traff. Startled, Zohra followed the sound in search of its source.

"What that?" she called to Gramma pointing to an object on the trunk.

"You know very well is Miss Omega, you see she plenty times already. Now say good afternoon."

When Zohra realised the voice came from a human being, she ran to hide behind Gramma.

"Stop hangin' on. You humbuggin' me from gratin' coconut. Miss Omega never bite you before."

The being on the trunk roared with laughter as Zohra peeped at her.

"She even fatter than Ismay," Zohra thought.

One could forgive the child for thinking that Miss Omega was strange. That lady seemed a human clothes horse. Miss Omega had tied a huge headkerchief round her head. It resembled a headless bird with half open wings.

"Come here, sweet-gal," the thick voice called.

Zohra clutched at Gramma.

"Why you frighten of me?" Miss Omega asked coaxingly.

Zohra shook her head vigorously.

"She lil' bit shy at first," Gramma explained. "but once she know you, she never stop talkin'."

"O.K. but next time me come back from Nickerie, me will bring you plenty orange, darlin'." Miss Omega said. "You go come to me then?"

Zohra still refused to commit herself until Miss Omega returned a month later with the oranges. She was wearing dark clothes with yellow and red patterns. She put the oranges on her lap.

"Come here, chile," Gramma called. "Say thanks to Miss Omega fo' bringin' you orange."

Reluctantly Zohra came into the kitchen.

"How you do? Me sure you grow a few mo' inches since me last see you."

"Lost you tongue?" Gramma enquired, scrubbing away at a soot-covered pot in the traff.

"Me is well thanks." Zohra answered at length.

"Praise the Lawd!" cried Miss Omega, rocking with laughter. "The chile talkin'!"

Again Miss Omega's voice echoed through the room. This time it blended in with the crackling fire in the stove. A sudden distortion occurred in the child's mind. For one fleeting second, the laughing woman with the oranges in her lap seemed to resemble the stove with its vermillion fire in the grate. Zohra started to giggle.

"Miss Stovie Omegie, Omegie-Stovie!" she cried.

"What you say?" Gramma asked. "Me hope you not rude to Miss Omega?!

"You callin' me names, chile?"

"No."

Miss Omega was not a stranger any more. Zohra had identified her with the stove. So when Miss Omega lifted Zohra on to the trunk beside her, the child did not object.

"Here you oranges!" Miss Omega laughed merrily, emptying the oranges into Zohra's lap. The little girl laughed and wriggled trying to catch them as they rolled about.

"Do it again!" Zohra cried, leaping off the trunk to pick up the last orange.

"Catch!"

She squatted with her back against the kitchen door, then sent the oranges hurtling across towards Miss Omega.

"Spare me, chile. Me too ole fo' bend down."

Zohra persisted, but as Miss Omega did not respond, the girl stopped to watch her. Minute beads of perspiration bejewelled her top lip. She began to fan herself with a handkerchief.

"The place so hot, Omega. Take some coconut water before you go," Gramma said.

"Thank you, Babe. But here the rent before me forget. Four dollars exactly. God, me fryin' in this heat."

"Eh eh, Mrs. Fisul," a nervous voice penetrated the window. "Is Omega voice me hear?"

Gramma who was about to offer Miss Omega the coconut water winced, causing some of it to spill.

"Oh me God!" Omega cried, jumping up with agility that belied her weight.

"That woman is a stray cat. Why she don't stay in she own house? All she can do is run round gossipin'. Tell she me goin'."

Gramma placed the coconut water on the trunk and walked to the traff window. Zohra, anxious to see what Mrs. Kalamadin wanted, followed.

"She just goin', Aisha."

"Me hear Omega just back from Nickerie and as she there me thought me would ask if she bring back any Dutch bag fo' sell."

"She don't have any."

"Oh, tell she me comin' over anyway."

Before Gramma could reply, Mrs, Kalamadin's head disappeared from the next door window.

"She comin', Omega," said Gramma wryly.

"That fast mouth woman! Let she come," grumbled Miss Omega.

"Miss Omega, you still there?" the irritating voice called again.

"You didn't give me time to get away," Miss Omega grumbled fiercely like the caged fire in the stove.

"Hide in the bathroom, Miss Omega!" Zohra eagerly suggested, trying to join in the grown-up game.

"No, chile. Me will meet that bareface woman."

"Omega gone?"

A tall shadow fell across the doorway. It looked like a small bungalow on stilts. But it was only Mrs. Kalamadin with an orhni draped over her head and half way down her hips just above her skirt.

"Got news from Nickerie, Miss Omega?" she asked. "You ain't bring none Dutch bags? You see me brass-face daughter-in-law over there?"

Miss Omega visibly swelled larger. She started to drink her coconut water slowly. Gramma set about lighting the fireside. The air was filled with the splitting of wood as she divided bits of wood with her cutlass.

"Eh eh, what happen, man?" Mrs Kalamadin tried again. "Like you all don't want to talk to me?"

"You look like you got plenty to say, so we givin' you a chance to say it," Miss Omega retorted.

"No, no. How you get on in Nickerie?"

"Well, thanks."

"You bring anythin' fo' sell?"

"No."

"What about them orange here? They look juicy. You selling any?"

"They fo' the chile."

Zohra saw Mrs. Kalamadin greedily seize and smell an orange.

"Leave me orange alone! Is me own!" she cried.

Gramma looked up from her work.

"Mind you manners, Zohra. Come help me lay the wood in the fireside."

"Awright, chile," snapped Mrs. Kalamadin. "Police don't lock up people fo' smelling orange."

The woman sat by the fireside, her eyes devouring and recording everything she saw.

"So you didn't see me stinkin' daughter-in-law?" she said to Omega.

"Leavin' me son fo' another man. Hmm."

"Aisha, take care, the chile listenin'." Gramma interrupted.

"She too young fo' understand. That boy distress so much 'bout the shame that gal bring him. Me tell he from the beginnin' the girl bad, but all this love picture he see at Metro turn his head. Now he know I was right."

"Go play on the steps, Zohra," Gramma quietly said continuing with her work.

"No," wailed Zohra. "Me want to play orange with Miss Omegie!"

"What a fool the gal was! She family hardly got dahl and rice fo' eat where she come from. Then she marry, get two frock and couple bangle only fo' catch another man."

"Go outside, Zohra," Gramma ordered.

"Why me can't watch you all and hear her quarrel, Gramma?"

"One mo' word from you and Miss Omega will take all them orange back to Nickerie. Outside."

Zohra reluctantly went to the back door. She looked hopefully at Miss Omega. But that lady seemed too occupied with drinking coconut water to notice Zohra's banishment. So she shuffled to the back door to sit on the top step, out of sight but not out of hearing.

"Say somethin'," needled Mrs. Kalamadin. "Isn't you that take she in when she get away from we?"

"Look, me ain't arguin'."

"Eh, eh, you hear she? Omega ain't arguin' when she colleague with the gal."

"Don't bring Betti into you dirty business, woman."

"You witness she callin' me woman, Mrs. Fisul?"

Zohra knew Mrs. Kalamadin was growing angry. Her voice always squeaked. It had formed a part of the background sounds of Zohra's childhood just as the squeaking of the mice did.

"This is fun," Zohra thought, edging up to the back door to put her head round the corner. "She standin' up like she goin' to row."

Indeed, Mrs. Kalamadin had risen, her eyes smouldering like the fireside.

"Shut up, you empty bottle!" Omega threatened, "or else me will shut you up with this coconut!". She held up the coconut menacingly. "Me know that gal since she lil' like Zohra. O.K. is true her people poor, but they good. You think me would see she roam the streets when you good fo' nothin' son kick she out? You like anybody fo' treat you daughter so?"

"Eh, eh, the woman mad to insult me? Me didn't tell Baito to do that."

"You after the boy day in, day out to beat his wife. You ain't satisfy to make you husband laughin' stock, you got to punish the gal too."

"Me didn't instigate me son. And Kalamadin lazy. The gal lazy too. She does sleep late every mawnin'."

"What you expect, when she drunk husband beat she every night? What make she lose the last baby?"

"She slip and fall."

"Lyin' devil. People does get lock up in prison fo' makin' their wife lose baby."

Omega advanced on her opponent.

"Miss Omega will pound she to pulp!" Zohra thought. "Gosh she so big and strong."

"Aisha, go to you house! Omega, sit down. You all mustn't fight here." Gramma's sane voice cut the air coolly. Mrs, Kalamadin scowled and cowered. Omega harnessed her magnificent anger. And Zohra was very proud of Gramma's power over these two fierce elements. The rest of the details dimmed in the child's mind, but unconsciously Gramma emerged heroic.

Gramma's kitchen continued to be a little world where other figures dawned on Zohra's mind in rapid succession.

"Co-co-nut! Eh Babe! Where you Nani, gal?"

"What?" Zohra looked up. "You want Gramma?"

"Tell Nani me come with the coconut oil. Mssh, mssh, donkey."

The small woman reined in her donkey. She just seemed another object on the cluttered cart where slender milk cans and squat oil barrels combined to make her minute and inconspicuous.

"Gramma! Gramma!" Zohra shouted.

The milk woman wore a curious waistcoat trimmed in red and embroidered profusely with yellow flowers which seemed to wink at the child in the sunlight. On her head, a neat striped headkerchief made her respectable for the sight of Indian menfolk and completed her outfit.

"Gramma!" Zohra called again, bounding towards her as she came downstairs with the rice can. "I want a jacket like that."

"Yes, when you grow up, chile. Now let we see Bhowji. Mawnin', how you old man today?"

"Not so bad, Mrs. Fisul. That stroke hit him bad, but at least he can drag heself round lil' bit now. Still, me got to do everythin', even milk the cow."

Bhowji sighed, then swung down from her seat. Zohra drew nearer, intrigued by her nose ring.

"It don't move when she talkin'," the girl thought. "Maybe she wear nose ring 'cause she got cows."

"How much milk you want today, Babe?"

Bhowji's bangles and ankle rings chinked as she hauled the milk can forward.

"Three pint milk and two gallon oil. Any rice today?"

"Not plenty. Is so hard fo' load the cart now Bhaya sick. Times like this, me sorry we ain't got chil'ren fo' help. You lucky, Babe."

"Me not sure. If you get a lil' boy fo' help you, he go away at night time. You got to keep your own chil'ren all the time. Let me give you a hand with that bag."

"Me too!" shouted Zohra, clambering up to push the rice bag towards them.

"Take care, chile, take care," Gramma warned.

The women and child heaved the bag from cart to ground. The sharp morning sunshine daggered sunrays into their backs. Sweat broke out under their armpits, around their temples and backs as they opened the rice bag. A musty smell arose as they unleashed the pattering raindrops of rice into Gramma's tin. Next syrup-brown coconut oil oozed into bottles. The heat intensified.

"Bhowji sweat and the coconut oil smell the same," Zohra thought wonderingly.

Together, Bhowji and Gramma hauled the milk can over to the bottom step, then straightened up slowly,

"That done now, Bhowji. Me almost soak through with sweat. You goin' to come up and drink some swank?"

"If it ain't too much trouble, Babe."

"No."

So Bhowji entered Gramma's kitchen to rest. As she sat on the trunk to drink her swank, Bhowji undid her ghoutri, or pouch. Coins clinked onto her lap.

"How much money you got, Bhowji?" cried Zohra, rushing over. "You ghangri look like it made outa copper."

The woman recoiled startled, hugging her skirt to her bosom as though Zohra had caught her in a secret act.

"This is big people business!" she cried fiercely. "Go play."

Wounded Zohra retired to the window by the stove, watching Bhowji from there. The woman stared back at her until Zohra became embarrassed and looked away. Gramma, who was peeling plantains, appeared oblivious of all these exchanges. Zohra could hear the clink of coins but whenever she met Bhowji's eyes, Fagin could not have regarded Oliver more fiercely than the woman did.

"How she playin' with the coppers just like we play marbles," Zohra thought. "Why?"

For half an hour Bhowji played greedily with the coins as she drank. Then reluctantly she poured them into the ghoutri again, tightly drawing the string.

"Me goin' now, Babe. Me will come back in a fortnight."

"O.K."

Then the woman went leaving behind the trailing wail of "co-co-o-nu-ut!"

"Why Bhowji does play with she copper so much, Gramma?"

"You got eyes like cat, gal."

"But why, Gramma?"

Gramma gathered up the plantain skins and considered Zohra for a while.

"Can you keep a secret?"

Zohra nodded eagerly.

"Bhowji love money,"

"That why she hide the ghourti when me look?"

"The woman frighten. Tell me chile, why me lock up flour in the trunk?"

"From the mice?"

"She lock up money same way from thiefman. And now she gettin' ole, she even afraid o' lil' chil'ren."

"Chil'ren?"

"Yes. But how you can understand?" Gramma said thoughtfully. "You too small. Ole age make you so lonely. Bhowji ain't got no chil'ren, and she husband half-dead. All she got is them copper. Me so sorry fo' people like Bhowji and even Aisha Kalamadin."

"Me don't like Mrs. Kalamadin. She quarrel too much."

"Look, when Baito married, she frighten he goin' to leave she. So she chase his wife from the house. But now Baito blamin' she. So she roam round quarrellin'. And that Bhowji, now she ole man sick, she hoardin' up all the money. Eh, eh, why me tellin' you all this? You is still a chile. Well me better strain rice now."

"Oh Gramma, it sound like Nansi story. Tell me why Boyie sell crush ice."

"Poor Boyie," Gramma said, removing the steaming rice pot from the fireside and fetching it over to the traff. "Don't come too near in case it slip and burn you."

Gently the old lady tilted it so that the water, or mar, issued from the closed lid into the traff.

"Tell me 'bout Boyie," Zohra persisted.

"He give his chil'ren all his money. Now they wash their hands on him. The trouble start because he make a will before he dead. That was he fault. So they kick him out of the house."

"That is why he does sell crush ice?" Zohra asked.

Gramma nodded and in Zohra's mind rose the vision of Boyie stooped almost double, pushing his cart. He sold crushed ice between midday and three o'clock when the sun was hottest, and even cane-cutters had a siesta. The child had never seen anyone perspire so much. Rivulets of perspiration ran from forehead to temples, channelling their way to his chest and back until his shirt lay like another moist, steamy skin against him.

"Poor Boyie," Zohra murmured, thinking of the perspiration, rather than Gramma's words.

"Eh, heh, is true Boyie poor now. His chil'ren use him like this traff. They strain out all his strength in the same way me strainin' this rice-mar down the traff. But God see everythin', chile. As long as me live, Boyie will get food from this house." Gramma's voice sank away sadly. Zohra touched her. "Mind the rice-pot, baby. Go play now. It ain't fo' long. You will grow big so quick."

Though Zohra could not fully appreciate the weight of Gramma's words, the people who visited the kitchen gained new dimensions. They were no longer strangers but unhappy people needing kindness.

"So that why they come," Zohra thought wonderingly. "Because Gramma kind. Gosh, me didn't know that before."

And slowly, Gramma's kitchen grew into many mansions which the little girl began to discover.

3. Miss Gusta's Lil' School

Capa's house looked on to the main road of the village. Each day she watched the bara lady selling bara and chutney to cinema-goers. She saw Mrs. Kalamadin squabbling with people in the shop, and their grey donkey returning from the wharf laden with sugar sacks. None of these interested her as much as Miss 'Gusta.

Zohra had admired Miss 'Gusta long before personal contact and the smell of guavas ripened their acquaintance into friendship. She passed Capa's house every Sunday on the way to church flanked on either side by a sister. The two Misses Braithwaites seemed to protect Miss 'Gusta from the onslaught of vulgar eyes as they walked along the road. Miss Joycelyn's near-sighted squint discouraged people. So did Miss Esther's dignity as she rose above her two sisters surveying the world with awesome detachment. Miss 'Gusta walked sheltered between them.

"Oh Miss 'Gusta look so nice in her crinoline hat and her stockings shining like dew," Zohra would say in wonder.

Each Sunday at eight o'clock, Zohra anxiously awaited Miss 'Gusta by the front window.

"They coming!" her voice rang out sure as a Gospel singer each week. "I can see their lace dress by the sweetie tree!"

The Misses Braithwaites dressed alike. The older sisters wore their clothes grimly like a challenge – a glove flung in the face of the world. Mss 'Gusta tried to follow suit, but femininity permeated her clothes in the way she wore her belt or pinned the flowers on her hat. Even at middle age, her eyes showed a girlish vulnerability that her sisters appeared to foster and guard.

Early in their acquaintance, this expression had appealed to Zohra's imagination, long before she succumbed to the luscious guava scent that surrounded Miss 'Gusta.

One day as they passed on Sunday, Zohra spoke to them.

"Mornin' Miss 'Gusta!" Zohra cried as the sisters neared Capa's house.

They paused to look down.

"Eh, eh," Miss 'Gusta answered. "You grow big, chile. You don't think so, Sis Joycie?" She turned to her sisters, pleading for agreement. "What you say, Sis Essie?"

The other two sisters nodded.

"The chile growin'," Miss Joycelyn agreed.

"Say howdy to Gramma for us," Miss Essie said.

"Thanks," Zohra said, overburdened with this honour.

Then she spent the rest of the day happily telling everyone about the sisters.

So when Zohra heard she was going to attend Miss 'Gusta's Kindergarten, she awaited her first day impatiently.

"Me goin' to Miss 'Gusta's school," she boasted to her friends in Long Range Yard. "Everyday I will see her crinoline hat and lace dress."

But Zohra was disappointed. Miss 'Gusta wore a stiffly starched cotton dress and her hair in woolly plaits.

"Oh Miss 'Gusta," Zohra said as soon as she arrived at the school. "What happen to all your nice clothes and stockings?"

Miss 'Gusta looked startled.

"But that's me church clothes, chile."

"Why you only wear them for church?"

"We should only dress up for the Lord. Who else should we dress for?"

"I did think you wear those all the time."

"No, no dear. Come on. We calling register now."

Miss 'Gusta put an arm round Zohra and took her into the house. By this time, the ravishing smell of ripe guavas drifted from Miss 'Gusta to distract Zohra, quenching her desire for that lady's beautiful clothes and silencing further enquiries. Zohra was happy to live in Miss 'Gusta's guava atmosphere.

At the kindergarten, each sister had a chore. Miss 'Gusta said prayers and taught the children. Miss Joycie saw the children do their exercises and inspected their nails while Miss Esther sat with the naughty ones after school. Each morning the routine followed the same pattern.

"Mawnin' chil'ren," Miss 'Gusta said.

"Mawnin' Miss 'Gusta."

"Now let us pray."

During the first week of school, Zohra prayed "Allah bless Mommy, Aunty, Henry, Gramma………."

"Our Father which art in heaven," prayed the class.

"Why Mommy didn't teach me that one?" Zohra thought.

Each day the question arose in Zohra's mind, but as she wished to fit in with the rest of the class, she adopted their version of prayer and pushed aside puzzling questions.

After prayers, Miss 'Gusta usually told Bible stories. She told her favourite "Suffer the little children to come to me" very often.

"The Jesus say 'Suffer the lil' chil'ren to come to me,' but only if you good He will say that to you. Is them chil'ren who say prayer, honour they father and they mother and love they neighbour who He will take to them green pastures in heaven. If you do these things, you will live on honey and manna fo' the rest o' you everlastin' life, Amen."

This outburst forced Miss 'Gusta to stop for breath.

"Who is Jee-sus?" Zohra would think. "Only Allah livin' in heaven."

"And the Lawd say you must love everybody, chil'ren," Miss 'Gusta would continue, emanating guavas and comfort. "Even people you all don't like. Love them, then life not hard fo' you. But Lawd Jesus!" she closed her eyes in ecstasy. "Adore He! Beautiful Jesus dyin' on the cross. Look at His shinin' face and side bleedin', yet He smile and love everybody. Nobody can help lovin' He, we Saviour, we King."

Her words seldom meant much to the children, but at these times, Miss 'Gusta radiated love and conquered them. The class sat spellbound, some sucking their fingers, others half-asleep and the rest open-mouthed. Even Zohra's puzzlement about Jesus disappeared in her love for Miss 'Gusta.

Nor did Miss 'Gusta domestically swerve from the theme of love and obedience that she preached. Miss Joycie usually grumbled about the children's dirty nails and runny noses. One afternoon she erupted in the middle of an Arithmetic lesson.

"Lucille and Chandra, you stayin' in this afternoon. Look at you nails. You too Frankie. What you mother give you a kerchief for? Blow your nose, boy!"

Lucille began to whimper. Miss 'Gusta's annoyance at this interruption revealed itself in the way her chalk squeaked on the blackboard and the rapid suppression of a frown. Then a look of sweet mildness spread over her face.

"Whatever you say, Sister."

Once Zohra heard Miss Essie dryly complaining when she and Frankie were playing bus drivers on the verandah. Miss Essie stood with her back to the nearby classroom window.

"You know me catch Mickey peepin' at Lucille pants yesterday. It ain't decent. Maybe we should ask them parents to make them wear long dresses."

"Chil'ren just lil' curious," Miss 'Gusta gently explained.

"But we mustn't encourage them to think bad things from that young,"

Zohra heard Miss 'Gusta sigh.

"You think we should write a letter to them parents and ask that the gals wear long dresses?"

There was another pause.

"Awright Sis Essie. You bound to know best, after all, you mind me ever since me lil'. You older and wiser."

This conversation resulted in a letter to each girl's parents asking them to dress their children in longer clothes. So Miss 'Gusta's girls came to be nicknamed lil' Mother Sallies because their long clothes reminded people of Mother Sally in the Christmas masquerades.

Somehow Zohra adapted herself to the Misses Braithwaites' school. She enjoyed the distinction of being called 'lil' Mother Sally'. The nickname made her feel she belonged to Miss 'Gusta. As Zohra grew to know her teacher, she also developed an ambivalent attitude towards religion. At school, she accepted the Trinity, thinking of Christ as the handsome, romantic hero of a film whom Miss 'Gusta loved. At home, Allah remained the stern, just Being who demanded retribution for naughtiness and answered prayers if one sacrificed pleasant things.

But Zohra found lessons the most interesting change in her life, for Miss 'Gusta spoke of the alphabet as though it were something deliciously edible.

"'A,'" said Miss 'Gusta "for a-a-p-le that you eat at Christmas time. And 'B' for b……..? What Gary Sobers does play cricket with?"

"Bat! Bat!" the children would shout.

"Now spell it!"

The class would triumphantly spell the word.

"And 'C'? C-c-? Tell we Claudie."

"Cat! Is a cat!"

"Yes just like Tabby. Tabby! Mssh, mssh! Come show them how you look, Tabby."

Tabby bounded up, rubbing his head against her legs.

Zohra felt a spurt of jealousy.

"He too must like the guava smell," she thought.

The days fell back like the read pages of an endless book, piling one on the other. Zohra's imagination expanded under Miss 'Gusta's care. Ordinary objects began to live new lives and after a while, she incorporated the things she saw in an alphabet of her own. She began to act Miss 'Gusta before the wardrobe mirror, wearing her mother's hat as well as an old lace tablecloth round her shoulders.

"'A' for what, Mickey?" Zohra asked her image, imitating Miss 'Gusta's voice.

"Ant eater." She spoke like Mickey.

"B-b-b- for what, Lucille?"

"Belly!" Zohra imitated Lucille's tone.

"Now listen, you all. 'C' for calabash like them in Long Range yard. 'D' for donkey like Kalamadin donkey. 'E' for eddo that Madeen always rootin' out. You hear me?"

This new alphabet delighted Zohra so much that she began to yell it at recess. Soon the children rejected their current favourite:

"Arithmetic, arithmetic, me father sick,

Me mother gone to Crabwood Creek!"

They took up Zohra's new alphabet. Miss 'Gusta soon felt the repercussions of Zohra's imagination.

"'G' for.....?"

"Guana, miss," cried Bebi; she meant iguana.

"Yes dear. But what else it mean?"

Bebi looked crestfallen.

"G-r-a-," Miss 'Gusta spelt hopefully.

But Zohra had unwittingly brainwashed the others.

"Grass! What happen to you all? Start again. 'A' for.....?"

"Ant eater."

"No, no! Apple that you eat at Christmas. And 'B' for.....?"

"Belly!"

Miss 'Gusta's head jerked up at the mention of that part of the anatomy which she delicately called 'tummy'.

"No, bat. What about 'D'?"

"Donkey."

"Good. 'E'?"

"Eddo."

"'E' is for egg, egg, you hear? Remember?"

They looked blank.

"Don't tell me I wastin' me time with you."

"But we forget, Miss," Claudie explained.

"Why?"

"Well, Zohra been tellin' us new a, b, c."

Miss 'Gusta's face hardened into the texture of dead mango leaves.

"Why you makin' so much mischief, Zohra?"

"Me just say it at playtime and everybody want to know."

"Awright. Stay in after school this afternoon and tell me all 'bout it."

Everyone stared at Zohra for Miss 'Gusta seldom kept anyone in after school.

"What's wrong?" Zohra thought. "Why she vex with me?"

At recess, instead of joining the other children on the verandah, the girl slunk away among the lime and guava trees. The stiff cleanliness of scrubbed boards and starched clothes which used to make Zohra feel at home grew suffocating. She felt refreshed and safe among the trees. Zohra scrambled up on the lowest branch of a guava tree.

"Is so nice here," she breathed. "It smell just like Miss 'Gusta." She frowned. "Why she so vex with me when me like she so much?"

She watched sunlight trickle through the gold dust enhancing spiders' webs, mellowing limes and colouring her skin tea-brown. Zohra's upper lip and palms began to perspire. Her unhappiness oozed away. Still, thoughtfulness remained clinging to her mind as the moss did to the trees.

"School-bell ringing." Zohra thought. "Miss 'Gusta will vex even more if me don't go."

At three that afternoon, the other children left Zohra sitting on the back bench, outweighed and dwarfed by her school bag. She still clutched her pencil-box, snapping it open and shut. Suddenly the box fell, disturbing Miss 'Gusta who had been marking slates.

"Me didn't keep you here fo' make noises. Pick it up and keep quiet."

Her stern voice demolished the little girl's courage. With tear-blurred eyes Zohra tried to collect her pencils. They lay on the floor, scattered rainbow of colours. Slowly, the child gathered her pencils, confining them as she had done earlier with her imagination. She began to crack her knuckles.

Miss Joycie entered, bringing in a glass of swank for her sister.

"Eh, eh, is first time you keep in Zohra," she said.

Miss 'Gusta looked up.

"She been teachin' them chil'ren the wrong alphabet."

"Oh, you bad lil' gal!" Miss Joycie cried. "Wait till Miss Esther hear this. Essie! Sis!"

"Wait a minute," Miss Essie said from the kitchen.

Zohra shivered.

Miss 'Gusta quietly sipped her Coca Cola while Miss Joycie cleaned the blackboard. Zohra watched the particles fall from the blackboard. They fell as dizzily as she had done from Miss 'Gusta's favour.

"What you all want?" said Miss Essie as she came from the kitchen. Her head, borne up by her long body, seemed to move among the rafters. Slowly, she lowered her eyes to her sister's level.

"What happen?"

"Mrs. Fisul grand daughter been teachin' them chil'ren wrong alphabet."

"Me never see the like in me born days, Sis Essie! She sit so quiet, then bam! She do this," Miss 'Gusta blurted out. "Messin' up all me hard work. How Anglican school will have them chil'ren if they don't know alphabet?"

Miss Esther lowered her eyes considerably more to Zohra's level.

"Come here, chile." Miss Esther said.

Zohra raised her scared eyes to Miss Esther's face. Mr. Brocklehurst never seemed so tall to Jane Eyre as Miss Esther seemed to the child in that moment. A few minutes earlier she had felt like chalk falling dizzily downwards. Now a reversal took place. This see-saw of emotion stupefied her. She went to the three sisters.

"Repeat the alphabet for them," Miss 'Gusta ordered.

Zohra's mouth opened but her voice refused to sound.

"Come on. You holler it at play time. Show we how you clever," Miss 'Gusta persuaded.

"Go on," said Miss Joycie.

Miss Esther alone remained aloof.

Zohra tried again. She began at 'A' and continued till her voice choked at 'I'.

"'J' for jamoon," she croaked. "'K' for kiskadee."

The words became muffled. Tears tumbled down her cheeks.

"Home......Mommy! Me want to go home!" Zohra cried.

"Why you cryin'?" Miss 'Gusta asked softly. "We ain't beat you. You got to learn you mustn't spoil other people work and make mischief. You all know sisters, how me live fo' the Lawd, you all and the teachin'. Now she spoil everythin'."

Though she was upset, Zohra sensed the hurt in Miss 'Gusta's voice. Then Miss Esther intervened.

"Quiet, 'Gusta," she commanded. "Sit down Zohra; wipe you eyes with this kerchief."

Then she turned to her sisters.

"Me surprise at you colleaguing with 'Gusta, Joycie. She is a big woman now, but still spiteful like lil' chile. She get vex because Zohra teach them chil'ren something they like more than she own. 'Gusta you think teaching is playin' dolly house? You think chil'ren is plaything?"

"Mind what you say in front the chile, Essie."

"Is best she learn while she lil', Joycie. Zohra you keep all you hear to yourself. You hear me?"

Zohra nodded, mopping her eyes with Miss Esther's handkerchief.

"You hurt Miss 'Gusta feelings tellin' them chil'ren new alphabet. You mustn't do it again, O.K.?"

"No. Me didn't know. Oh, me like Miss 'Gusta, oh!" she began to cry again. "She always look so nice in she hat and stockin' and lace....."

"You ain't sorry, 'Gusta? Isn't you who always talking 'bout 'suffer the lil' chil'ren?" Miss Esther demanded.

Miss 'Gusta looked upset.

"Oh, Sis Essie!"

"And.....and she always smell so nice, like guava....." Zohra blubbered.

A low laugh halted the child's tears. She looked up. Miss Esther was laughing quietly, her tall frame shaking like the lime trees and her all-seeing eyes shut. Zohra stopped crying for she had never seen Miss Esther laugh. The child felt as though she were in the presence of a great phenomenon such as an earthquake or flood.

"Guavas!" panted Miss Esther. "Man, that beat everthin', 'Gusta!"

Her body folded up like a deck chair as she sat next to Zohra. The other two began to laugh.

"Well," said Miss 'Gusta at last. "We better get you some of Miss Joycie nice sponge cake. Wait here."

Miss 'Gusta's eyes once more projected love. Zohra nodded happily.

"Zohra," said Essie gently when her sisters had quitted the room. "Me believe chil'ren must learn young. They is lil' grown-ups. You see because Miss 'Gusta like teaching, she don't like anybody to interfere. So she vex when you teach them chil'ren the alphabet, but she too proud to see this. So she vex. Me don't know if you can understand."

Zohra's eyes grew larger; she still clutched Miss Essie's handkerchief and grimly tried to understand. Miss Esther looked at her kindly.

"You make a good alphabet, but wait till you turn big to teach it." Then she added almost to herself: "God send the chile to protect we from pride. Is true He say except you be lil' chil'ren, you can't enter the kingdom of heaven. He teach we this all over again."

"Miss Essie talkin' bout God again. But she so nice and make Miss 'Gusta like me again," Zohra thought.

Miss Esther's eyes encountered the child's at that moment. She smiled, but unlike Miss 'Gusta's smile, hers contained no vulnerability. It was similar to the protection and the strength the trees in their garden offered that morning.

4. The Threat

Zohra felt more grown up than the children at school and at home because Miss Esther had confided in her. She was impatient with her younger brother, Nizam, who frequently disturbed her play. One day he snatched her doll and ran away with it. When Zohra caught him, they fought over the doll. Nizam pulled off one of the doll's legs and Zohra hit him. He began to yell.

Zohra ran to hide behind the kitchen door. She felt safely wedged in by wood there. Nizam's yells ceased and her mother rushed into the kitchen.

"Where's she hiding?" her mother cried.

Gramma's hands stopped in mid-air over the traff. Droplets of water darted sunlight as she hesitated.

"Behind the kitchen door," she said.

"Come out, Zohra," her mother commanded.

"No."

"Yes. Come here at once. Ain't you shamed o' youself?"

"No."

"Why you hit your brother?"

"He pull off dolly leg."

"Come here."

"You will beat me."

"No."

Reluctantly Zohra came from her secure fortress of wood into the unprotecting kitchen.

"I tired of this behaviour, Zohra," said her mother, shaking her. "Why you can't treat your lil' brother nice like you treat Henry or people in Long Range Yard?"

"They is me friends."

"Nizam is your brother."

Zohra could not answer. Her mind was full of conflict. He always tore her books or upset the furniture in her doll's house or filled up holes she had dug in the backyard. He never seemed to understand if she just spoke to him.

"Now the chile bawlin' his head off and givin' me headache," her mother complained.

Zohra began to feel guilty. She twisted the hem of her dress.

"Stop that," cried her mother. "No wonder you got holes in your clothes. Is hard enough to make ends meet."

The child's hands dropped limply to her sides.

"Is enough now," Gramma remarked quietly.

"Times like this she is a real devil. I got a good mind to send her back to her Daddy."

Zohra froze. This threat was the worst thing that could happen to her.

"No, please Mommy."

"Wait till New Amsterdam bus pass at one o'clock," threatened her mother. "I goin' to put you on it."

"Me won't go!"

Zohra saw her father rarely. On those occasions, she kissed the strange man and sat awkwardly on his lap. The child's thoughts usually followed her mother who never remained in the room. Her bitterness after the divorce prevented her from meeting her husband again. Now the strange man with his wide eyes and clean white shirt rose before her. Zohra felt very cold.

"Me don't like him."

"Is your father," her mother said. "Is his turn to try and understand you for a bit. You past me understanding."

"Gramma, tell Mommy not to send me away!"

In Zohra's mind, her father lived nowhere. He appeared suddenly on the doorstep like a weed which had sprouted overnight. Zohra could imagine him nowhere else. Besides, the thought of leaving Capa's house, her back yard, the cinema, and all her friends crushed her completely.

"Go upstairs and lie down for a bit," Gramma suggested to Zohra's mother.

"She not sending me away?" Zohra asked.

Neither woman answered. They looked as inscrutable as cloudless skies in the dry season. The child crept from the kitchen. A well of sorrow rose deep as the vat in the backyard and seemed to submerge her. Everything outside was charged with strangeness. The shadows cast by the sour-sap tree were ghostly at midday. Red sawdust on the muddy earth looked like blood. Even her lifelong companion, the sun, penetrated her shrinking flesh with needles of sunlight. She felt these familiar things had rejected her as her mother had done.

"Why it wrong to hit Nizam if he break me dolly?" she wondered.

The twelve o'clock whistle from Skeldon sugar factory blew. It sounded lonely in the vast sky. Zohra shivered.

"Soon the bus will pass," she thought. "I got to hide."

She stood in the sawdust in the middle of the back yard. She looked for a hiding place with the clarity that fear sometimes brings. The objects no longer blended into the background but become individual, complete parts of a whole. She saw the back steps with gaping slits like a sly, half-opened mask. The oblong gap between the kitchen and the cake shop dominated her. She walked towards this threatening space, and as she did so, remembered the storeroom on the left-hand side. The door had disappeared a long time ago. Old sacks of sawdust, dismembered parts of furniture and an old barrel stood in it. Above, filigreed cobwebs swayed, trapping breeze and sunlight.

Zohra stared at the storeroom as she had done many times before.

"It is so quiet," she thought.

She could hear the pad of feet in the kitchen above and faint disembodied voices. It looked inviting, so she went in. Her feet raised circles of dust. She touched the dislocated pole of an old brass bedstead and the rump of a faded sofa. The musty smell saddened and reminded her of her mother's threat. She peeped into the barrel. Sawdust half filled it.

A bus horn hooted on the main road, and this sign decided Zohra. She climbed on the old sofa, hung on to the brass pole and leapt into the barrel. The sawdust gave way as she landed softly. The particles produced a gentle tickling sensation against her skin.

"Is liyin' like roti-crumbs," she thought.

Another bus horn sounded. Zohra drew her legs against her stomach and looked up. She saw the barrel curved above her head. The bus passed and Zohra relaxed.

"How the cobwebs swinging," she thought, watching the sunlight on the roof.

Then she played a game with herself counting the cobwebs and guessing which shred the wind would blow away.

"Zohra, come and eat!" called her mother.

The child's body tensed. She hugged her knees.

"I ain't comin'," she whispered defiantly.

"Zohra," she heard her mother call. "Where that gal gone? She slippery like greasy pole. You turn you back an' she disappear."

She heard Gramma walk over to the kitchen door.

"Maybe she gone upstairs," Gramma said.

There were footsteps on the floorboards above and the clatter of kitchen utensils. Zohra moved slightly so that her feet would not go to sleep. More footsteps came.

"Me can't find she, Ma. I will go over to Long Range Yard."

Her mother ran down the back steps in a clatter of high heels. Bits of laterite brick crunched as she went over towards Metro Gap.

"Zohra! Oh, Sophie, you seen Zohra?"

"No, ask Ismay."

"Ismay, you see Zohra?"

"No."

"I wonder where she gone?"

"Try Henry."

Her mother's footsteps died away and she began to feel a different fear.

"Maybe she will vex with me when I come out," she said. "I better stay here a long time."

She listened intensely for her mother again. The cobwebs seemed to flicker endlessly before her mother came back. The tickling sensation of the sawdust became uncomfortable as the heat grew.

"Ma, she ain't there," cried her mother's voice as she ran up the back stairs. "I goin' to the cake shop."

Her mother came towards the storeroom. Zohra held her breath, but she passed on through the corridor to the shop. Then she heard her uncle's voice.

"I ain't seen her."

"Where she gone then?"

"You sure you look everywhere?"

"Yes."

"You search under the house?"

The house stood on small stilts. There was a gap between the floor and the earth under which a child could hide.

"Madeen, see if Zohra under the house," her Uncle said.

Zohra dug downwards into the sawdust, making a hole for her body.

"Madeen know this place, I must hide more," Zohra thought.

She heard Madeen scouting around and her mother going upstairs.

"Where she gone? She never late like this! Is almost one o'clock."

"The bus will pass just now, I got to stay here," Zohra thought.

At this point, she heard several voices. Footsteps sounded loudly on the kitchen floor.

"God, you don't think she gone to the beach and drown she self?" her mother cried.

"Zohra too sensible for that," her aunt replied.

"Maybe somebody carry she away," her mother said.

"Zohra! Zohra!" called her Aunt. "Come home, baby."

"I tell you she gone. Is no use calling," her mother wept.

Zohra felt as though they were mourning her death.

"Why Mommy cryin'? I only hidin' for a bit because she say she will send me 'way."

"Calm down," her aunt said and came downstairs to look.

"Sophie," she called. "We can't find Zohra anywhere. Look round Long Range for her, please."

"O.K."

Meanwhile her uncle and Madeen came out of the backdoor of the shop.

"You search everywhere, Madeen?"

"Yes, Mr. Fisul."

Her uncle paused. She could almost hear him thinking.

"You look in the storeroom?"

"No."

"Come on."

They came in and called her name. Zohra held her breath but they only looked round briefly and went away. By this time, Zohra's fear had grown worse. She not only feared being sent to her father, but her mother's weeping, a possible punishment and the fear felt when others spoke as though she had left forever. Upstairs the voices grew more excited.

"It's almost two o'clock now," her uncle said. "She been gone long."

Suddenly, Zohra realised that the bus must have passed. They could no longer send her away. She laughed. Sawdust flew into her mouth. She coughed. Zohra climbed out of the barrel, shook off the sawdust, then quietly went upstairs. Her mother sat surrounded by the family. Even Sophie had come over. Zohra stood in the doorway, awed by the result of her action. At first no one noticed her, then her brother looked up.

"Mommy, look! Zohra come back!" he cried.

Everyone looked towards the door. Zohra faced the barrage of stares guiltily.

"Where you been?" asked Gramma.

"Nowhere."

"My baby!" cried her mother, rushing over to hug her. "I thought you lost."

Zohra did not respond to her embraces.

"We look everywhere for you. Is past lunchtime."

"Me hungry."

"Tell us where you been."

Zohra lowered her eyes.

"Why you go 'way?" pleaded her mother, then she turned to the others in despair. "You see what me mean? She so secretive. Me can't understand she at all. What I do to make her behave like this?"

"Me hungry, Mommy," Zohra said.

Her mother shook her head, and Gramma walked over to the stove.

"We got hassar curry today. Eat something, chile."

"Awright."

She went over to the traff to wash her hands, then sat down to eat her lunch.

"Me don't care. I won't tell them where I been," she thought.

The family watched her silently.

"Me give up," her mother said at last and went away.

5. A Kite Like Christ

The rain fell, washing Long Range another shade of wooden silver and with it came Easter.

The children in Long Range Yard and Capa's house looked forward to Easter. It is the time of kite-flying. All shapes and colours of kites plumed the air. They were exotic birds sailing above the beach which Capa's house overlooked.

Each year the children had a sort of competition. They boasted how they would make the best kites. This year, Zohra did not join them. It seemed more important to find out why Guyanese people flew kites at Easter and why it was considered unlucky to fly them at other times. She stood by the window that night watching Aunt Jai in the rocking chair.

"Why we fly kites at East, Aunt Jai?"

"I ain't sure. Is somethin' Christian."

"Christian?"

"Me ain't sure. Ask Miss 'Gusta. She should know. She always go to church."

So the next time Zohra saw Miss 'Gusta, she asked about it.

"Why we fly kite at Easter?"

"Kite is the soul of our Lawd flying up to heaven when it rise at Easter."

"How He can fly when He dead?"

"He is the Son of God."

Miss 'Gusta said this conclusively as though it proved everything. But Zohra did not understand. She was Moslem, and they believed that Christ was a prophet. Yet Christmas, like Easter, had been made a public holiday. Hindus, Moslems and Christians celebrated it.

"Is Allah Christ Father?"

"Yes."

"But Allah is everybody Father."

"Yes, but Christ special."

"Why?"

Miss 'Gusta thought for a moment.

"He got special powers."

"Like Obeah Man?"

"No, different power."

"Because He magic? That's why He get up after He dead?"

"Yes."

"Like Sleeping Beauty?"

Miss 'Gusta looked confused, then said "Uh huh, lil' bit."

Zohra glanced at Miss 'Gusta's picture of the Good Shepherd above the table and tried to impress it on her memory. That Easter, the girl walked around carrying in her mind the vision of a beautiful pre-Raphaelite looking Christ with smooth hair. At first He slept peacefully, then woke up to fly to heaven. This vision impressed her so much that she decided to make a kite like Christ that Easter.

"What sorta kite you making this Easter, Amin?" she asked her cousin.

"Aeroplane kite."

"What kind you havin', Veronica?" she asked.

"One swordfish one."

"And you, Ricky?"

"Oh, a big one, so big, I will fly it with rope instead o' twine."

Zohra felt very pleased. No one had mentioned a kite like Christ.

"Now who can make kite and won't tell anybody?" she thought, thinking about her acquaintances. "Madeen too watermouth. Uncle Mus too busy. Amin too small. Now who will help me?"

The first week of her holiday passed while she thought about this problem. Her anxiety grew greater as the week before Easter arrived. Already her mother had begun work on Nizam's kite.

"You want a kite?" she asked Zohra, armed with bits of pointer broom, flour paste and gaudy tissue paper.

Temptation gnawed at Zohra, but the vision of Miss 'Gusta's Christ rose, rejecting any substitute.

"No." Zohra answered.

She started thinking again of people who could help with her kite, then suddenly remembered.

"Henry will do it. He don't talk too much to plenty other people. Maybe he can make it and hide it till Easter."

So she went to the cinema in search of Henry. Today he was mopping the floor.

"Henry?"

"I working."

"Yes, but I want to ask you something."

"Well, sit down in front row and put your foot up."

"O.K."

Zohra went into the front row of the stalls and sat down, drawing her knees up to her chin. Henry mopped the floor near her.

"Is Easter soon," Zohra began.

"Me know,"

"Henry, I got to make a kite."

"Oh."

"Me don't know how to make it."

"What sort you want?"

Zohra hesitated for a moment. "Maybe I shouldn't tell Henry till he promise to keep it secret and make it," she thought.

"It hard to make," she said aloud side-stepping his question.

""Well, make an easy one, then."

"Everybody making easy one."

"How you will make yours, then?"

Henry stopped his mopping to glance at her. Zohra looked down at the wet floor, then at Henry.

"You will help me?"

Henry stared at her with eyes deep as the womb-like cinema.

"Me don't know."

"Swear true true God, first, before I tell you."

"Who I can tell?"

"Promise, please."

"Awright," Henry sighed. "True true God."

Zohra jumped out of her seat and went to him. Then she whispered, as though afraid the very air might hear.

"Me want a kite like Christ."

"What?"

"Miss 'Gusta say we all fly kite at Easter because Christ fly up to heaven then."

"Whoever hear about kite like that?"

"Please help me make it."

"Me don't know how."

"Oh, you bound to know."

The child looked up so eagerly at him and her glance showed such implicit trust that Henry felt defeated. He lived alone and was only human. Zohra had kept him company ever since she could toddle to the door of the cinema. He could not refuse her.

"O.K., but we got to think 'bout it."

"Oh thank you, Henry, thank you."

Zohra embraced Henry and the mop stick. Though the water splashed his trousers, her gratitude sealed his promise.

"What this kite must look like?"

Zohra tried to describe Miss 'Gusta's picture.

"He got long hair like them men in that picture "Three Musketeers". You remember that? And he wearing this long nightgown. I got one at home. I can show you."

"You sure the man wearing nightgown?"

"Yes, and he magic like Sleeping Beauty."

"You not tellin' story, eh, Zohra?"

"No, no. Miss 'Gusta tell me."

Miss 'Gusta seemed too respectable a source to be doubted.

"Well, come back this afternoon after you done eating. We will see then."

Henry had just finished lunch when Zohra returned. His room smelt of dahl and rice. He emptied the ashes from his charcoal cooker outside the door as Zohra watched fascinated.

"Me been thinking, Zohra, it too hard."

"Oh, Henry!"

"Well, how we going to form the man head? Pointer broom too stiff. It will break."

Zohra thought for a minute.

"Let we use wire. Mommy got plenty. She make paper flower with them."

Henry straightened up and watched her for a minute.

"You want this kite bad, bad, eh?"

"Yes."

Henry looked at her thoughtfully.

"O.K. We make the head from wire and stick paper for the face. But how we will make the hair?"

"We can make it with twine. We can even make his nightgown with old cloth."

"It won't stick to the kite frame, gal."

"Let we use white paper."

A gorgeous paper Christ rose in Zohra's mind. He flew so high that no one saw anything but miles of twine.

"We got to get the paper first," Henry said.

"Yes, I got four cents."

"O.K. Here three cents more. Run over to Kalamadin store and ask for six cents kite paper and paste."

When Zohra had returned with these things, Henry had cleared a rickety table and broken up some pointers from his own broom. He sat arranging and re-arranging them like one absorbed in a difficult jigsaw problem. Zohra sensed his concentration. She put her shopping on the bed and watched quietly. Henry looked up after a few minutes silence.

"I thought you did run away, man."

"No, I watching."

"You know Zohra, you does ask for the moon sometimes."

Zohra was genuinely puzzled.

"Me can't remember that. I asking for a kite this time."

Henry smiled. "Me still ain't sure what he look like."

"I tell you already."

"Yes. Long hair and a nightgown. Don't sound like a man to me."

"Miss 'Gusta got his picture on the wall. She like him and does talk about him all the time at school."

"If only me had a picture."

"I wish I coulda borrow Miss 'Gusta picture."

But she knew Miss 'Gusta was too strict and would never lend it.

As Zohra tried to think of someone with a picture of Christ, she leaned against the table in her absentmindedness. All Henry's intricate patterns fell on the floor.

"Look what you done."

"I sorry."

She helped him pick them up.

"Me think Sophie might have a picture," she said. "I will go and see."

"Awright, go quick and leave me in peace."

She quietly crept away, then ran to Sophie in Long Range Yard. Even Sophie was indoors today. The sun shone so hotly that Zohra felt sure one could fry eggs on the zinc roofs. She saw Sophie mixing dough through the open door.

"Afternoon, Sophie."

"Howdy."

"What you makin'?"

"Hot cross buns."

"You ain't buying them from cake shop?"

"They too dear."

Zohra's eyes followed Sophie's swirling, floury fists.

"Sophie, what Christ like?"

Sophie stopped kneading dough.

"Why you want to know?"

"Is a secret. You got a picture of Him?"

"You not playing monkey with me?"

"I just want to see."

Sophie began to knead the dough thoughtfully.

"If I show you, promise you will only look, not touch."

"O.K."

"Wait till I done."

Zohra waited, shifting from one foot to another. Sophie's stern face encouraged no conversation today. She finished kneading the dough and carefully washed her hands in the traff.

"Come on."

Carefully, the washerwoman drew the curtain which divided the room into bedroom and kitchen. Sophie's mother was asleep on the bed. Above her on the wall hung a picture of Christ. His heart bled profusely under its golden haze and the mild expression in his eyes belied his bleeding heart. Zohra wondered at it all. He was different from Miss 'Gusta's Christ.

"Why He bleeding?"

"He suffering for all Mankind."

"Why?"

"He love them."

This made little sense to Zohra. She gazed at the picture, trying to decide whether she could help Sophie by cutting her finger with a razor-blade, and letting the blood flow.

"It will only hurt me."

Then she dismissed the subject. It seemed another superstition of the mysterious adult world she only half understood.

"You got any more?"

"Yes."

Quietly, Sophie went to the cupboard. A whiff of mothballs and Ricketts' Crown Blue bombarded Zohra's nose. The washerwoman drew out a framed picture.

"Look at our Lawd."

Sophie displayed the picture, speaking in a tone of great reverence. Zohra's blood curdled as she looked. A bleeding, sweating man lay on the cross with thorns on his head and nails in his hands. He bore no relation to the other two pictures she had seen. He was just an ordinary man on a cross suspended in the sky. Zohra felt afraid. She tried not to think how painful it would be. Would a man be strong enough to bear it? She thought of the only man she knew well.

"Henry would die if it was him."

Then she looked at Sophie. "That is Christ?"

"He suffering for we sins."

"He ain't the same man," the girl said looking once again at the Christ of the sacred heart.

"Yes, this is when He rise from the dead at Easter."

"Like Sleeping Beauty?"

"Don't mock we Lawd."

"I ain't mocking Him."

"I putting it back now."

Zohra only glanced at the picture quickly, trying to remember some of the less awful details for Henry.

"You can't lend that one to me?" she asked pointing at the Christ of the sacred heart.

"No, but you can look."

Zohra gazed at the picture, but all the while she thought of the blood and pain of the other crucified Christ.

"Me done now," she said.

Sophie put the other picture away and they tiptoed into the kitchen. For a few minutes they remained very quiet, then Zohra slipped away and went back to Henry.

He had tied together a sort of frame for the kite.

"Henry."

When he did not reply, she continued almost to herself.

"Sophie got two Christ."

"What?"

"You see, one bleeding and He ain't got on plenty clothes."

"You mean they different?"

"Yes."

"Well, which one you want?"

Zohra thought. The images of Christ – serene, knocking at the door, sentimental in Sophie's first picture churned in her mind. "The one with long hair and nightgown."

She could not bear to fly a naked, bleeding Christ. It would almost be like flying the bleeding chickens which her uncle slaughtered each week for chicken curry.

"Don't change you mind now. Run and get the wire for the head."

They spent the next hour cutting and pasting bits of tissue paper to the frame Henry had constructed. Then it was time for Henry to open the cinema for the four o'clock matinee.

"Promise you won't tell anybody."

"No."

"I comin' back tomorrow."

The next few days slipped by. The kite grew until it looked like a coloured glass mosaic ripped from a church window. Zohra became so excited, she could scarcely keep her secret any more. That night before she went to bed, she said to her mother:

"Mommy, Henry comin' to the beach with we on Easter Sunday."

"Why?"

"Is a surprise."

"You always hidin' things from me. Why he should come?"

"Please, is a secret."

"Me can't understand you. You refuse to make a kite this Easter, then now you want Henry to come with we. Why you don't play with you cousins? Why you got to play with big people?"

Zohra felt humiliated. "Amin and Nizam so small, they always breakin' up me things."

"You should love them as much as you love all them Long Range people you always runnin' about with."

"But is fun."

"Go to sleep."

Zohra lay awake a long time. She planned to run away if they did not allow Henry to come. When at last she fell asleep, she dreamt of Christ flying in the sky at the end of a piece of twine.

"Henry!" she called. "It ain't too heavy for the twine. Look, it flying."

She laughed and her laugh echoed from horizon to horizon. She looked about, but there was nothing except endless beach and rive. "Henry!" she cried. Again her voice bounced off the horizon.

"I lost, Henry!" She let go the twine. Suddenly, out of the blue sunlit sky, a cross came plummeting downwards. "Henry!" she screamed. She grabbed wildly for the twine, but her screams fenced her in. The cross crashed into the sand. Zohra looked up. It stood upright against the rim of the world. On it, bleeding, nailed and crucified, lay a thin brown body.

"Henry, come down!" she pleaded. "Henry."
"What wrong, Zohra?"
"Is Henry."
Slowly her mother's face focused. In the background, she saw Gramma lighting the paraffin lamp.
"I thought Henry dead," she whispered.
"You been dreamin'", her mother comforted.
"He shoulda only make Christ, not go up on the cross."
"He ain't dead," said her mother. "Cock crowing. Is morning now. I just hear him open Metro gate."
Slowly Zohra realised that it had been a dream. Still, in her head, screams echoed in a world of sand where Henry lay crucified.
"What I tell you last night? You play too much with Henry."
But Zohra remembered the kite Henry made.
"Me love Henry, Mommy."
"Oh Zohra!"
Zohra felt the force of her mother's disapproval in these words and fell back in bed, turning her face to the wall. Later, she slipped away as soon as she could to Henry. With the dream still fresh in her mind, she had to find out whether he was still alive. Then she saw him emptying dustbins in the sunshine. An over-whelming burst of affection drove her towards him.
"Henry!" she shrieked.
He was still straightening up when she flew against him, rubbing her face on his shirt.
"What wrong?"
"Let we break the kite up!"
"After all the work we do, man?"
Zohra knew his reproach was justified. She loved him so much for being alive that she could deny him nothing.

Next day as soon as she awoke, she begged for Henry should come. At last she told her secret in order to persuade her.

"He make a kite for me."

"Oh."

"Please Mommy, only Henry know how to fly it."

Eventually her mother gave way under this battery of requests. So Henry brought the kite to the beach. It was just across the road from Zohra's house and most of the people from Long Range Yard were there. Henry unwrapped the tail from around the kite. Its string hair lifted in the wind and the robe fluttered.

"What the meaning o' this?" demanded Sophie when she saw it.

"That's why me wanted to see you picture." Zohra said.

"What picture?" her mother asked.

"She ask me to see a picture o' Christ. Is because she want to make this."

"Zohra!" said her mother sternly.

"But Miss 'Gusta say Christ rise today. Me did only want to make him fly to heaven.

"Lawd," Sophie said softly. "Chile, I don't know how you think about all these things."

The children from the yard came to inspect the Christ kite while Zohra stood uncertainly by Henry.

"You got a man with a red stain on his chest," Veronica commented.

"Is Christ," Zohra said,

"Eh? But where His halo?"

"Don't make sport o' we Lawd." Sophie cautioned. "Is blasphemy."

"What you got there!" shouted Ismay. She approached with a baby astride her hip. "Don't tell me so! Lemme see. Is His heart."

She laughed, and taking a cue from her, Zohra's mother smiled.

"You got a gal and a half," chuckled Ismay.

Zohra seized the opportunity and made Henry raise the kite. It ascended in the afternoon sun. He gave her the twine.

"That done, now," he said. "I going."

"No, stay."

"Why?"

"Then I will be sure only the kite will fall outa the sky," the child said referring to her dream and holding on to his trousers with her free hand. Henry seemed puzzled, but Zohra sighed happily. "Nobody else got a kite like Christ."

6. Pigeon Stew

Easter was over. Everything else seemed an anti-climax after the kite like Christ. Gramma had just ordered Zohra out of the kitchen because she had been playing with the lighted wood in the fireside. Zohra went downstairs slowly, dragging each foot against the steps.

She stared at the ground. It had rained hard the previous night and many puddles pocked the backyard. Zohra looked at them thoughtfully, then got her spade from the storeroom. She began to dig a valley between the puddles, draining the water from one to another.

"Hey Zohra!" Madeen called.

But Zohra was too busy to answer.

"Guess what, man?"

He pulled her hair.

"Leave me alone. You can't see I busy?"

"You go be so vex if you don't listen."

Zohra did not answer, but dug on.

"I got two pigeons."

"Where?"

"Pa send them to your Uncle Mus."

"What he goin' to do with them?"

"Eat them."

"But he can't do that."
"The white one too beautiful, man."
"He can't kill nice pigeons."
"Wait and see if he don't do it."

Zohra stopped digging and watched Madeen uprooting eddo plants from the trench near the house. Green eddo leaves fell, palette-shaped and smooth. Driblets of water slid off them into the water. They lay in a row, like a dead army before the firing squad of Madeen's hands.

Madeen was about twelve years old and came to help Uncle Mus on Saturdays in the cake shop and around the yard. Zohra knew he felt superior because he was a boy. Though his shirt lay paper-thin and ragged on his back, he assumed he knew more than she did.

"Why we got to eat pigeons?"
"Because we got to live. Why gal so stupid they can't understand?"
"We ain't stupid. Anyway, boys stupid too, cat-eyes!"

This insult irritated Madeen who dropped the unfortunate eddo plant in his hand.

"Plop!" it went in the mud as it fell.
"Plap! Plap! Plap!" went the children's feet as Madeen chased Zohra from the trench.

He hated being called cat-eyes. This term was one of abuse for the sprinkling of Guyanese who were the illegitimate ancestors of European overseers on the sugar plantations.

"Wait till me catch you, gal!"

Zohra abandoned her shoes which stuck fast in the mud and ran shrieking to the cake shop where her Uncle Mus sat reading the 'Daily Chronicle'. She could never remember him without it. He looked up.

"What happening?" he asked. "Why all the noise?"
"Madeen chasin' me!"

Zohra headed through an opening in the counter and grabbed his legs for protection.

"Why you chasin' she?" demanded Uncle Mus.

"She call me cat-eyes, Mr. Fisul."

"Eh, eh fire-flint what you do that for? You won't like it if he tease you."

"But he say girls stupid. That why me call him cat-eyes."

"Look here boy, me ain't payin' you to make trouble. Go back to you work. You Zohra, stay here or go upstairs to you mother."

"Me want to stay here," Zohra said timidly.

When Madeen had left, she looked at her uncle.

"You goin' to kill them pigeons, Uncle?"

"Yes, for dinner."

"Me don't want any. Why we can't just keep them fo' eggs like the fowl?"

"Too much work for Gramma."

"Then let we give them to Henry. He can keep them behind the stage."

"No. And stop asking too much question. Keep quiet or go upstairs."

So Zohra chose to be quiet and stood by the glass case on the counter. She watched the ants fight a losing battle as they tried to reach the legs of the case so that they could eat the cakes within. Uncle Mus had placed the legs in old sardine cans full of water. The ants crawled up the cans first, then unaware of the trap, fell into the water. To Zohra, this death by drowning appeared an elaborate game. The ants were so alike and had little individuality. But the pigeons were different. They had eyes, made soft sounds and would bleed like Zohra if they were killed. She hated the idea of it all, but felt afraid to broach the subject again with her uncle. So she slipped away, past cartons of Coca Cola piled under the counter, bulls' eyes bottles and boxes of straw.

Outside, she looked for Madeen. He had rooted out most of the eddo plants. Now he squatted in the shadow of the house, looking as vanquished as the fallen eddo plants.

"Madeen!"

He stubbornly contemplated the uprooted eddoes.

"Please listen, man."

"No."

"Yes, yes. Look, you make me vex just now. Girls ain't stupid. Hear."

"No. You call me cat-eyes."

"You tease me first."

He turned away and yanked out a few blades of grass.

"If you steal them pigeons, me will give you twelve cents."

Madeen's head shifted slightly in her direction.

"Twelve whole cents. You can buy sling-shot and red-bread."

Madeen's profile could now be seen.

"Me will even give toffee I got from Henry."

The temptation was too great. Madeen faced her squarely now.

"O.K. Is a bargain. One thing more."

"What?"

"Say you like me cat-eyes."

"O.K. Me like you cat-eyes."

"Anyway, how me will get them pigeon back, eh Zohra?"

"Where you put them?"

"In Gramma fowl pen."

"That easy, we goin' to open the pen."

"O.K."

So the children set off for the chicken run by the bulging water vat. Softly, they crept behind it and hid under the sour-sap tree until they were sure no one had seen them. Madeen tried the door of the coop, but Gramma had locked it. They could see the pigeons fluttering within but could not reach them.

"The white one lovely," Zohra said, pressing her face against the wire mesh. "Let we take it away."

"But the thing ain't openin'."

"Break it."

"You uncle will tell me father and he will lick me."

"Yes. Oh, what we goin' to do, Madeen?"

They sat under the sour-sap tree sadly. The twelve cents seemed an eternity away to Madeen. Zohra felt certain the pigeons would die. They sat for a long time trying to think of a way out. Then Zohra leapt up.

"Red ants bite you, man?" Madeen asked.

"Listen. When Uncle killing them pigeon?"

"Four o'clock."

"Well, me give you another twelve cents for keeping Uncle in the shop at four o'clock."

"How?"

"Oh, fool him 'bout somethin'."

"But suppose you Uncle find out?"

"Oh hurry up Madeen!"

She ran up the back steps leaving Madeen to carry out his bit of the plan. Upstairs Gramma sat on a massive wooden trunk in the kitchen kneading dough for roti. She looked up as Zohra entered.

"Where you been?"

"Oh downstairs."

She watched Gramma for a while, then spoke again.

"What we havin' fo' dinner?"

"Pigeon stew and roti."

"Where…..where the pigeon?"

"In the fowl pen."

"Me want to see them."

"Not till dinnertime."

"Please Gramma."

Gramma looked at her shrewdly for a moment.

"Is better if you don't. Now don't argue, I got work to do this afternoon."

So Zohra was forced to be quiet and stay with Gramma till four. Then the old lady went to the chicken run.

"Madeen! Madeen! Go call Mr. Fisul."

Madeen appeared, nodded at Gramma and disappeared towards the front of the house.

Gramma took out her ghoutri and pulled out a bunch of keys. Zohra watched as she opened the door. The old lady put her arm inside and grabbed at the fluttering pigeons. At this moment, Grip who had followed them, began to bark. Mistaking the pigeons for his old enemies, the hens, he tried to get into the coop.

"Shh, go 'way Grip!" Gramma scolded. "Hold him Zohra! Where that gal?"

Zohra had disappeared. She hid behind the vat, and Gramma pushed the door to without locking it as she chased Grip off. Zohra darted to the coop, wrenched open the door and clawed wildly at the white pigeon. She grasped some feathers and drew her hand out. She had rescued the white pigeon. She looked about her, just in time to see Gramma's skirts. Then she fled up the backstairs and up through the kitchen, past the bathroom door, and up to her bedroom. The pigeon flapped unhappily.

"Shh, pigeon. Don't make noise," she coaxed gently.

Softly, she opened the door of the room and ran to the open window by the wardrobe. She was on the verge of hurling the pigeon out, when her mother called.

"Why you at the window? You ain't flyin' pillow-cases again?"

Zohra smothered the pigeon closer, hiding by the wardrobe, so her mother could not see her. Then she panicked and shoved the bird into the tiny space between the wardrobe and the wall. She came forward quickly and held out her empty hands.

"Look. Nothin'"

"Me thought you had somethin' white in yo' hand."

"Was nothin'."

Half her mind willed the pigeon to stay quiet; the other half willed her mother to believe her. The child felt her freedom, Madeen's and the pigeon's were at stake. Her mother checked the window and satisfied herself that there was nothing there. Miraculously, the pigeon remained quiet.

"Keep quiet one minute more, lil' pigeon," she begged as she listened intently. "Nobody comin'. Is O.K. Now me will take the money from me puzzlin' tin fo' Madeen,"

Zohra pulled out her piggy-bank from under the bed and began to extract the twelve cents from a narrow slit in its side. She fumbled alternately rattling the tin and cautioning the bird.

"I see she do it!" came Gramma's voice.

"Shh pigeon," Zohra whispered.

"But she didn't have it, Ma," came her mother's voice.

When they entered, Zohra looked up smiling. Some coins lay on the counterpane.

"Zohra, where that pigeon?" Gramma demanded.

"I don't know, Gramma."

"I see you run upstairs with it."

"I don't know."

"Uncle waitin'" her mother said. "If you did take it from the coop, give it to Gramma."

"What that?" Gramma cried, jerking her head in the direction of the wardrobe.

And sure enough, Zohra could hear the ill-starred pigeon signalling to its hunters.

"Is only mice." Zohra shook the coins in her piggy-bank to cover up the sounds.

"Since when mouse start flappin' about?"

"Stop rattlin' that box. You givin' me a headache," said her mother.

They hurried over to the window, followed the sound and soon discovered the pigeon.

"Don't kill it! Don't kill it, please!" screamed Zohra.

"You naughty gal. Now we got to shift this wardrobe," complained her mother.

Together they heaved the wardrobe forward while Zohra watched them.

"Why me can't buy it from you for twelve cents?" she begged. "Take twelve cents, Gramma."

They appeared too busy to hear her, but at last Gramma emerged with the pigeon. It was slightly greyer for its experiences. Gramma's stern face silenced Zohra as she marched out of the bedroom with the bird. The child cast herself down and wept.

"Why you cryin'?" her mother asked. "Don't get on like that. Me head killin' me."

"Why you all got to kill it?" Zohra demanded through a tear storm.

"We got to eat it for dinner."

"But it bleed like we, Mommy. Tell Uncle not to kill it."

"It won't feel anythin', baby."

"But the pigeon will squeak hard! The blood will fall all over the place."

"We got to eat, Zohra. Maybe if you run down and ask Uncle, he won't kill it.

Zohra ran to the door, then hesitated.

"Me can't go," she said shame-facedly. "If Madeen see me been cryin', he will think I stupid."

"Maybe if you powder you face with some talc, he won't notice."

So her mother put some talc on her face and a few seconds later Zohra ran downstairs to her uncle.

At the bottom of the stairs, she stopped. There before her lay both pigeons, blood oozing slowly from their throats. They were very dead. Around them stood Uncle with the dripping knife, Gramma, Madeen and Grip wagging his tail.

7. Onion And Garlic

The land on the banks of the Corentyne River is below sea level. Before they built the sea wall or dyke to keep out the river, it crept under Kalamadin's shop and slurped over the main road. The Long Range children and Madeen had fun sailing boats in the water. Zohra was not allowed to share in the fun.

"You might fall in the trench and drown," Zohra's mother had warned.

So Zohra watched her friends longingly from the window.

Before the sea wall had been built, the Local Authority dug trenches or gutters parallel to the road to drain river water and excess rainfall. Most shops and houses along the road had little bridges over these trenches leading to the road. When the dry season came, the trenches dried up and eddo plants died. It was then the reign of carrion crow bush and black sage. Green lizards scuttled along dry trenches disturbing nothing but dead leaves.

Occasionally, Zohra would hide under Uncle Mus' cake shop bridge while playing hide-and-seek or watching wood ants. That day she crouched under the bridge watching the long tunnels built by the wood ants. Sometimes the bare sole or shoe of a customer would be seen through the boards of the shop bridge. Slits of sunshine zebraed across the earth under the bridge and Zohra lay back against the bridge post. She held a brittle twig ready to break the tunnel. As the bits from the tunnel fell, forming a hole, ants gushed out running madly in all directions.

A sudden grunt from the trench startled her. She crept up to look. Sunshine slit the bundle of rags that lay there in sections. Only the eyes in one section moved. A hand shot out from the bundle and covered the eyes. Zohra fell back against the bridge post in fright. Onion and Garlic froze in the trench.

"Is a Jumbee Baby," he thought. "I will lie quiet, quiet. Maybe it will go 'way."

He held his breath and pressed his fingers to his eyes, but when he looked again, the thing had re-appeared.

"It got hair like black snakes," he thought, terrified. "God save me."

The hair swung back and once again the Jumbee Baby disappeared in a rustle of leaves. He waited tensely, but when nothing happened, Onion sat up and looked about him.

"What you doin' there?" a voice brayed.

Onion looked up.

"Oh me Gawd! Is a jackass!" he thought.

"Uncle Mus," said the Jumbee Baby. "Is only Onion and Garlic."

"I know. Get out from under me shop bridge," Mus commanded.

"How it brayin'" thought Onion as he picked up his sack and tried to scramble out of the trench. "I can't find the Corentyne. Somehow I in a bad country where there just animal and Jumbees."

"Lemme catch you here again and me go teach you a lesson!" shouted Mus.

They watched the bundle of rags grovelling in the dust of the trench, clinging to carrion crow bush to gain the road.

Early in the morning some weeks later, Mus was reading his 'Daily Chronicle' when Zohra burst in.

"Uncle Mus! Uncle Mus! Kalamadin want to talk to you!"

Mus raised his head still full of half-digested newsprint, and focused on his niece.

"You mean 'Mister' Kalamadin, hotmouth," he said. "Is manners to call big man ole enough to be your father, Kalamadin?"

"Awright, Mr. Kalamadin want you. Come quick."

Mus went on to his shop bridge and shouted across the road to Kalamadin.

"What wrong, man?"

"Come see, Mus."

Mus crossed the road followed by Zohra and went to the gallery or verandah of Kalamadin's shop. The only unsightly thing on the scrubbed floorboards was a bundle of rags with a head and limbs sticking out of it.

"Is Onion and Garlic," Zohra whispered in awe. "You think he weary?"

"Me don't care if he weary, what to do, Mus?" Kalamadin pleaded. "Two, three days now the place stinking and only today I find him."

"Kick him out, man; is your property," Mus advised.

"The man mad. Me frighten him."

"Get Police Fernandes. He will do it."

"You think so?"

"Yes."

"But he might die if you lock him up," Zohra said.

"You always meddlin' in big people business," Mus growled.

Zohra ignored his comment. She knew he became like this if he was worrying about something, and he was certainly worrying about Onion and Garlic. He thought he was a nuisance which should be removed.

"O.K. Me will call Fernandes. Stay here in case Aisha come. You know what she like."

Mus nodded. Everyone knew how quarrelsome Mrs. Kalamadin was. While Kalamadin ran off for the village constable, Zohra stayed with her uncle and peered at Onion and Garlic. The children at school gave him his name. Whenever he appeared, they would chase him away chanting:

"Onion and Garlic pound Massala!

Onion and Garlic pound Massala!"

These two ingredients went into every passable massala curry in the village, and the name stuck to the ragged man.

"Why you think they call him Onion and Garlic, Uncle Mus?" she whispered.

"I don't know. Maybe is to do with his smell."

"What he got in the bag?"

"Some people say he got plenty money there."

"He is a rich man?"

"So they say."

"But why he ain't got a house?"

"His head ain't too good."

"You mean he mad?"

Uncle Mus nodded. His temper was improving, so Zohra asked him more questions.

"Other madmen roaming round besides Onion and Garlic?" she asked.

"No, they lock them up in a lunatic asylum."

"Oh," said Zohra. "They must frighten bad."

"They mad. They don't feel like that."

"How you know? You been inside the asylum?" asked Zohra without realising the irony of her question.

"Man, Zohra," Uncle Mus said. "Sometimes you does ask some funny questions."

Mus was becoming impatient with her again. So she turned to Onion and Garlic. He hugged his sack tightly in his sleep. His hair and beard were full of little bits of vegetation picked up from days and nights sleeping in the open. Zohra crept round him noticing the bandages on his ankles and the toughness of his soles.

"You mad, too?" Uncle Mus cried, when he realised what she was doing. "Move out. He might wake up and grab you."

But Uncle Mus' urgent voice had woken Onion and Garlic. He muttered, rubbed his eyes and looked at Zohra. They stared at each other in amazement.

"Uncle, he wake up," Zohra whispered.

"Move quick from there!" Mus cried in alarm.

Onion and Garlic shut his eyes tightly.

"It happening again," he thought. "The Jackass braying and Jumbee Baby staring at me. Oh Gawd, let them go away."

Zohra was heavy. She could not move. Mus strode over and wrenched her away from near Onion and Garlic.

"Your Gramma will blame me if anythin' happen to you, Zohra. Move away from here!" Mus said, then looked at Onion.

The man sat up and fumbled with the string at the neck of his sack.

"I did warn you before to get off other people property," Mus said sternly.

Onion paid no attention to him, but concentrated on the knot of the string.

"Now, stay behind me, Zohra," Mus warned. "Don't go near in case he got cutlass in the sack."

But Onion and Garlic only brought out a little framed picture from the sack. They could not see whose picture it was, but as he placed it before him, he began to sway backwards and forwards.

"Omm. Omm. Peace," he chanted to himself. "Lord Khrisna, omm. Help me get outa this hell."

Mus caught sight of the picture. He looked worried.

"Zohra, stand on the shop bridge. Oh me Gawd! The man working obeah. Run quick and tell Kalamadin, chile!"

Zohra, who had been eagerly observing the tramp as well, said "Me think he praying, Uncle. Benje did that one time."

"Why you never listen, eh fire-flint?" Mus exploded. "Why you always tellin' me what to do when you should be doin' what I tell you. Run quick and get Kalamadin."

Zohra ran off to meet Kalamadin. She dodged donkey carts and cane-cutters on bicycles. She saw the shopkeeper and constable by Goldsmith Deen's jewellery shop. Red puffs of dust at their heels kept time with their gasps as they ran.

"Hurry up, man," Fernandes was saying.

"Me trying," grunted Kalamadin, trying to propel his eighteen stone body at the same rate as the constable's lean one. "Give me a chance!"

"Come quick, Kalamadin – oh I mean Mr. Kalamadin," cried Zohra. "Onion and Garlic doing obeah on your gallery."

"Gawd," bawled Kalamadin. "If Aisha come round to the gallery, she will murder him."

The men ran on, leaving Zohra behind. When she reached there, more people had gathered to watch. Mrs. Kalamadin had discovered the blot on her clean floor.

"Eh, eh, look me trouble!" she wailed. "Look what happen to me clean, clean floor."

Onion and Garlic sat swaying backward and forward.

"Oh, Khrishna, Ram, help me," Onion prayed. "Them Jumbees gettin' nearer."

The noises outside him became louder.

"Get up, man!" shouted Fernandes. "You trespassing,"

"Don't holler too much, Fernandes," begged Kalamadin. "He might make big obeah and spoil me business."

"They shoulda lock him up long ago in Canje Lunatic Asylum!" cried Mrs. Kalamadin.

Kalamadin turned round as though he had been whipped.

"Shut you mouth woman."

"You all see how he quarrelling with me?" shouted Mrs. Kalamadin.

"You shut up. Don't forget is my father who buy this house and business. Me ain't lettin' you spoil it."

"Eh, eh, Mrs. Kalamadin," said Mus, trying to calm her down. "If you talk too much he will do worse obeah."

"He might even strike you dumb," said Kalamadin, needled by his wife's comment about money.

Mrs. Kalamadin glowered at them, but remained silent. Zohra would have giggled if she had not been so disturbed by Onion and Garlic. She could hardly believe Mrs. Kalamadin's silence.

Now Fernandes squatted before Onion and his picture.

"Look," he reasoned with Onion. "Me is a policeman. I tellin' you to leave Kalamadin shop."

As Fenandes' voice penetrated Onion's consciousness, the man opened his eyes. He stopped swaying and put his hand before him to ward off the sight of Fernandes. The constable sprang back, thinking Onion was about to attack him. He lost his balance and sprawled on the floor. Someone in the crowd tittered. Onion's eyes fastened on the policeman's body dressed in black.

"I pray to you, Khrishna," he thought, "and you send me Jumbee Bird all black to kill me. And they talking, talking all the time like people but looking like spirit."

"You blind or somethin', eh?" Fernandes demanded angrily. "You can't see me is the law?"

He moved in on Onion who grabbed his picture and held it before him to ward off the evil Jumbee Bird he saw.

"Me go lock you up," Fernandes said menacingly.

A gentle breeze blew in from the Corentyne. Onion's stench floated towards the onlookers. Everyone drew back, but it proved too much for Mrs. Kalamadin.

"You stinkin' chamar!" she shrieked. "Get up!"

Mrs Kalamadin rushed at him. Onion braced his back against the wall still holding the picture before him for protection.

"Is the Jumbee itself," he thought. "Help me, Khrishna, all them gods help me."

"What wrong with you, woman?" cried Kalamadin, trying to restrain her.

"Leave me alone," she said, pulling away her arm.

"He really praying, Mrs. Kalamadin, he frighten," Zohra pleased.

"If me take away his picture," Mrs. Kalamadin said, "he won't do no obeah."

"Don't do it, Aisha," begged her husband.

But before anyone could stop her, she had snatched the picture from Onion and Garlic.

"What you done?" Kalamadin whispered in horror. "You touch obeah thing!"

Onion and Garlic felt the picture go and saw the fiery eyes of the Jumbee Lady. He knew she was a spirit of the dead by her eyes and contorted face.

"Now if this Jumbee get away with the picture, how Khrishna will forgive me now I loss the picture?" thought Onion. "He will put me in hell."

Mrs. Kalamadin stood hesitating with the picture at Onion's eye level. Her hand drew him like a magnet. He felt that he would be forgiven if he retrieved the picture. The crowd watched as his great hand clamped down on Mrs. Kalamadin's arm.

"All you help!" she yelled. "What you police for, Fernandes?"

Fernandes rushed forward and grabbed Onion, trying to make him loosen his grip. But Onion would not.

"Omm. Jai jai jag-a-ray," he prayed to himself. "Vishnu, Rama, all you got gie me strength."

Kalamadin tried to pull his wife free, but Onion's grip tightened. No one had ever thought he possessed such strength.

"Drop the picture, Mrs. Kalamadin," Zohra begged. "Is the picture he want."

But by this time, Onion leaned forward with a mighty effort and sank what remaining teeth he had in Mrs. Kalamadin's arm.

"Ow, me dead!" cried Mrs. Kalamadin, forced to drop the picture.

Fernandes heaved Onion against the wall as he clutched his picture again. "Get some rope. We got to tie up the madman."

Onion felt pain but his terror of being surrounded by the animals was much greater.

"Protec' me from Jumbees and wild animals," he prayed. "Look how me get back your picture, Khrisna."

A crowd of cane-cutters on their way to work had stopped to watch. They still had their food carriers and cutlasses.

"She shouldn't ha' done it, man," said one of them. "Now Onion put obeah on she."

"Oh me Gawd!" shrieked Mrs. Kalamadin. "Me will go mad with madman bite."

"Is your own fault, woman," said Kalamadin whom she had pushed away from her. "Shut up, or I will burst your mouth."

"You can talk so now you use me up and me money," wept Mrs. Kalamadin.

Kalamadin rushed at her, infuriated by her insults, but Mus grabbed hold of him. In the confusion, Fernandes slackened his grip on Onion who ran forward. He seized his sack and battered his way through the crowd. Everyone scattered. Zohra hid behind a flour sack and the cane-cutters ran into the trench.

"Jumbees! Animals!" cried Onion, speaking for the first time.

People looked at each other. They had always thought he was dumb as he had never spoken before. A cane-cutter waved a cutlass at him.

"They will chop me up," Onion thought and hobbled away as quickly as his feet would carry him.

He saw great stones whiz past him. Red stuff dripped from his forehead, but he clutched his picture for protection. A few minutes later the Jumbee bird descended on him, tying his hands. The picture went flying in Kalamadin's trench during the struggle.

"Omm. Peace, Lord," prayed Onion. "Why them devil tormenting me?"

He had no time to find the picture before they bundled him into a truck and drove off.

When everyone had gone, Zohra quickly went into the trench where she had seen the picture fall. She slipped it into her pocket. Onion felt it was years later when the truck stopped. The Jumbee bird swooped on him and took him to a big cage with an iron gate. Then he knew the gods had not forgiven him the loss of the picture.

"Is a jail," he said, looking at the iron gates. But when he saw the animals grovelling inside and heard their cries, he knew he was in hell. For the first time since they knew him, his captors heard Onion and Garlic shout. And his roar was louder and more terrifying than all the other patients of the Canje Lunatic Asylum where he had been admitted.

That afternoon, along under the cake shop bridge watching wood ants and sun zebraing though chinks in bridge boards, Zohra drew out Onion and Garlic's picture. A blue Khrisna played his flute in green fields.

"Don't worry, Onion and Garlic," she said. "When you come back, you will get back your picture. They wouldn't ha' let me give it back to you because they scared of obeah."

Zohra looked at the part of the trench where she had first discovered him asleep.

"You was praying," she said gently, "I know, 'cause Benje pray like that."

Carefully, she wiped the picture on her frock and returned it to her pocket. Then she began to make holes in the wood ants' tunnels.

Zohra kept the picture for years but never heard of Onion and Garlic again. He disappeared from the village like flood water from the Corentyne River. The same river water never flooded the road twice. Different water comes each year, and different people entered Zohra's life dimming the memory of Onion and Garlic.

8. The Masqueraders

The year spun on towards Christmas. The dry season gave way to the rainy season. Zohra learnt to write at school and to forget Onion and Garlic. She began to write lists of presents she wanted for Christmas.

A few days before Christmas, Zohra helped Henry cut a huge branch from the flamboyant tree behind Metro. They fetched it back together up the stairs to the sitting room in Capa's house. The branch seemed like a massive insect half asleep on the floor. Its leaves looked like hundreds of tiny feet reflected in the mirror of the polished floor.

Zohra lay on her stomach close beside it. She could see the branch and its reflection on the floor.

"It crawlin' like a big centipede, Mommy," she observed, as her hand crept along pretending to be a spider attacking the centipede.

"You will get cold lyin' there," her mother said. "Get up and help me break off them leaves." Zohra got up to help. They stripped the branch until it was skeletal.

"Bring that crepe paper," said her mother.

Zohra ran over to the box. Vivid colours splashed out from it, dazzling her. Trembling, she took out a few rolls. Her excitement mounted. Christmas had arrived. Christmas was

A Guyanese Family

the colour and texture of crepe paper, the smell of Mansion polish blending with sponge cakes, the music of masqueraders and rain drumming on roofs. But most important of all, Christmas was the time of Santa Claus and presents.

"Now fold the paper so and cut," said her mother when Zohra had sat down beside her. Zohra clipped away at the paper letting her mind wander to Long Range Yard. Benje's grandson Fredrick would be practising with his band. They had just bought a new drum and planned to collect more money masquerading this year on Christmas Day.

"Come Zohra, let's put on some leaves," said her mother, recalling her to the present. They began to cover the naked branch with crepe paper foliage to give it the appearance of a real Christmas tree. Gramma came in.

"Don't it look nice?" she said.

"Will you hold the branch, Ma?" Zohra's mother asked.

Gramma held the branch steady in the best jardinière while Zohra's mother crumpled newspaper round the base to hold the tree firm. When they had finished, it leaned against the wall almost six feet high and looked more like a green flounced skirt than a Christmas tree. But to Zohra it looked like a real Christmas tree.

"Better leave it to dry now," Zohra's mother said.

Zohra admired the tree once more, then went over to Long Range Yard where Fredrick was practising with his band. All the children had gathered around to be entertained.

Fredrick stood waving his arms about.

"Come on, man. You all ain't dead. You knockin' the drum as though you already in your coffin. And Basdeo, the flute made for blowin', so for Gawdsake blow it!"

He walked round his musicians alternately coaxing, encouraging and bullying them.

"Now fo' the march. O.K. Fenton and Jackson, begin."

The steel drums tinkled away, ice cool on a warm day. The children followed the musicians round Long Range Yard as though they were the Pied Pipers of Skeldon.

"Stop!" yelled Fredrick. Everyone stood still.

"You know what you all look like?" asked Fredrick quietly, walking round his musicians like a sergeant major.

They murmured among themselves.

"A bunch of ole fowl cocks who loss their combs!" he hollered. "Fenton, you will dress up as a woman, so fo' the Lawd sake dance like a woman. Jerk you hips, man."

He walked up to Jackson.

"Eh, eh, Jackson, since when you dancin' by yourself. You dancin' with a lady, so look at she, man."

He took the two youths and placed them before each other. Then he turned to the children.

"And you all chil'ren, if you don't want me fo' tan your hides, sit on the steps."

He pointed to the steps and all the children slunk away there reluctantly. They knew Fredrick meant business. Soon everyone was ready for rehearsal again. Even the children sat quietly ready when Veronica suddenly broke the silence.

"Hey Fredrick, stop quick. They comin'."

"I swear I will give you licks like peas now, Veronica!"

"No, no Fredrick," said Veronica dodging him. "Look, is Big Boy,"

Immediately the group broke up. All the youths disappeared to hide the instruments and only Fredrick remained. The children cowered behind him. Big Boy had arrived. He towered six feet of rippling black muscle and quite dwarfed Fredrick.

"Eh, eh Fredrick man, what this me hear?" he said softly.

"What you hear?" Fredrick asked roughly.

"The boys at Mus cake shop say you havin' masquerade this Christmas."

"Me thinkin' 'bout it."

"You think as much as you like," continued Big Boy softly, then he yelled at the top of his voice, "But Lawd help you if I meet you on the road."

The children ran away to hide and even Fredrick moved back a few paces.

"Is a free country," Fredrick said.

"We been doin' this area fo' years. Now young fowl cock like you think you can take over. Take care."

"I hear you got a new drum. Take care you don't lose it."

Fredrick walked straight up to Big Boy.

Veronica and Zohra began to shout in unison, "Fredrick, come back! Come back!"

"You touch me drum and I will murder you."

Big Boy laughed.

"You really makin' me laugh."

The children sensed a fight. Veronica tried to pull Fredrick away. He brushed her aside like a fly. The men rushed at each other like fighting cocks. Zohra ran for Sophie. Everyone knew that both men were in love with Sophie and this really caused their hostility. Big Boy had struck the first blow when Sophie arrived.

"We don't want mad dogs in Long Range Yard," Sophie said. "Move out quick sharp before I call police."

"Aw, Sophie," said Big Boy, "is only a friendly argument."

"Friendly like snake and mongoose, eh?" Fredrick retorted. "This blood on me face look friendly?"

Big Boy scowled at Fredrick but dared not argue.

"I don't want to hear anythin', just move out and leave us in peace," Sophie commanded.

Both men slunk away under the fire of Sophie's eyes. When they had gone, Sophie returned to beating clothes with a vengeance. Zohra watched the sprays of soapy liquid fly through the air. Sophie seemed so absorbed and remote that Zohra felt she was imprisoned in the soap bubbles.

"Sophie, ain't it nice now Christmas comin'?"

It was as though Zohra had pressed a button to slow down a machine. Sophie's arm became slower. She spoke from arcs of spray.

"Yes."

"We got a Christmas tree," Zohra said. "Me aunty baking Christmas cake and patties. And with Fredrick new drum we should have lovely masquerade this year."

"If Fredrick don't watch out, Big Boy will give him coffin for a Christmas present."

"People don't die at Christmas."

Sophie smiled at Zohra's innocence and Zohra felt close to her again. The washerwoman lay down her clothes beater.

"Look, I know our Lawd born at Christmas, but since this is a sinful world, people sometime die too."

"Oh, nobody must die. We goin' to be very happy."

"Well," said Sophie, when she saw the worry on Zohra's face. "Maybe God will make a special exception this year."

Sophie began to hang out clothes.

"I savin' up money specially for Fredrick masquerade," Zohra confided.

"Don't waste you pennies on Fredrick, chile. He and Big Boy only doin' it to get money fo' rum shop."

"But I know Fredrick like music," Zohra protested.

She could feel his joy and excitement when the band performed well. Zohra believed his music was to him what crepe paper was to her. To Fredrick his music meant Christmas.

"Why Sophie can't see how me and Fredrick like Christmas?" thought Zohra.

"Anyway," said Sophie as she began to wring a fresh load of clothes. "What Christmas got to do with masquerading? Hand me the Ricketts' Blue."

Zohra passed her the blue. She crumbled the cube in a bucket of water and immersed all the white clothes in it.

"Is a serious time to think o' Baby Jesus born in the world and thank God for Him. What jump-up music got to do with it? You should be joyful in church not brawlin' in the street like Fredrick."

"It ain't the same," Zohra said.

She could not explain the conflicting emotions within her. It was the same as Miss 'Gusta's school. Zohra was not Christian although she knew Jesus, yet she shared Christmas Day with Christians as it was a public holiday. Zohra felt glad that Jesus had been born. His birth gave her an opportunity to enjoy Christmas and the masqueraders. There would be no Christmas for her without these things. Fredrick was a nominal Christian and for him masquerading meant Christmas. His joy in song and dance was born again like Jesus at Christmas. At this time, he changed from a rowdy loafer to a spirited man with a purpose. As she could not express her feelings adequately to Sophie, she changed the subject.

"Guess what I gettin' fo' Christmas?"

"What?"

"Dolly and pram from Santa."

"You got to be a very good gal to get such nice present."

"Well, Amin really bad last year and still he got present. I better than him, so I should get dolly and pram."

"I hope you right."

"What you gettin', Sophie?"

"Not dolly and pram, man."

"No, what big people present you gettin'?"

"Not much."

"But you must get somethin'."

"Me too ole."

"But Gramma gettin' somethin' and she older than you."

"We will see."

"I will write to Santa Claus specially for you."

Sophie paused from her washing to laugh.

"Why you laughin'?" Zohra asked.

"Don't worry you head, darlin'"

"You think Henry gettin' anythin'?"

"Henry will manage. We all manage somehow round here."

"I will write a letter for Henry too."

"You too soft-hearted, chile. Take care people don't take advantage of you later on."

Zohra hardly heard her.

"Maybe I will ask Henry," she mused.

Zohra left Sophie thoughtfully. She stepped through Metro Gap and went up the red laterite path to the cinema, climbed the familiar steps and walked through the half-shuttered doors. Only dust stirred in the womb-like shadows of the cinema.

"Henry!" she called.

"Henry!" echoed the empty seats.

"You not there?" she asked.

"You not there?" came the cavernous reply of the cinema's unseen being.

Zohra walked out into the dazzling sunshine again. She skirted round the cinema to the back where carrion-crow bushes projected bulbous yellow lamps of flowers and black sage smell calmed the fevered air. The door to Henry's room stood open. A film of smoke misted the air and masked the cinema's caretaker.

"Henry?"

"Yes?"

"I can't see you."

Slowly a brown hand came up and waved away the smoke.

"Is only smoke."

The smoke cleared and Henry reappeared sitting on his chair.

"Henry, you gettin' anythin' for Christmas?"

"I don't know."

"I sure you been good this year, Henry. You should get a present."

Henry's face lit up in amusement for an instant.

"I ain't been bad," he said.

"What you want? I writin' to Santa."

"I leave it up to you. You ask fo' what I need," replied Henry joining in her game.

"No, tell me."

"You see 'bout it."

"You want a surprise then?"

"Yes."

"I goin' home to write now. 'Bye 'bye."

She waved goodbye and ran out into black sage air, singing like a Kiskadee and dancing to the imagined rhythm of Fredrick's drum. When she reached their backyard, Madeen, who had been sweeping the yard, looked up. It was his day to help Uncle Mus.

"What you hollerin' for?" he asked.

"Is Christmas. I writin' to Santa Claus."

"There ain't nobody like that, stupid."

Madeen's respect for girls had not been heightened by knowing Zohra. Once when Zohra had decided to save the pigeons, he thought she might be clever. But then she hid one behind the wardrobe and Gramma found it. She had given him twelve cents. He only took this as a sign of weakness.

"She too stupid," he thought.

"'Course there is. I got presents from Santa before," Zohra was saying.

"How come I ain't got none?"

"Maybe you ain't been good enough."

"What you mean?"

"Well, you not nice to anybody. You pull Grip tail and make him bark. You call me stupid, and steal Uncle Mus ice cream. How you can expect to get anythin' from Santa?"

"Take care!" he cried and began to chase her round the vat.

"Leave me alone! Stop it!" she cried.

"Don't holler!" hissed Madeen. "Uncle Mus will hear."

"Stop chasin' me then."

He stopped and leaned against the vat.

"I got to go and write two letters to Santa," panted Zohra.

"Letters?"

"Yes. You write and ask Santa for things at Christmas."

Madeen looked at her suspiciously.

"True, true," Zohra protested.

"Well," said Madeen cunningly. "You can prove Santa Claus really there if you get me a train set for Christmas."

"O.K. I bet you."

And Zohra marched upstairs defiantly. She took her mother's writing pad and wrote letters to Santa asking for three presents. Then she enclosed them in envelopes, decorated them with her version of hibiscuses and coconut palms and hid them behind the wardrobe to await Christmas Eve.

That night the rain came. Zohra awoke to its tattoo on the zinc roof.

"Maybe Santa Claus send the reindeer to dance on the roofs."

So as the storm raged, pulling at jalousies and pelleting windows with raindrops, Zohra lay in her bed secure in dreams of Christmas. The next day she went to Long Range Yard to watch Fredrick rehearse. He was very upset.

"Man, if this rain continue, we will float about on Christmas Day like them animal in Noah's Ark," he complained to anyone who would listen.

"Oh, don't worry, Fredrick," Zohra said. "It bound to be nice on Christmas Day."

"Me won't bank on that," Fredrick grumbled. "Look at the mud on this yard. How we can practise here?"

The green had become a square of mud. Numerous barefooted children churned it up by walking on it. Fredrick started his rehearsal in an irritable mood.

"Fo' Gawd sake, stamp you foot, Fenton!" he growled.

"Look at the mud, man.."

"Don't look at the mud. You won't dance on glass on Christmas Day. Stamp you foot!"

When the children applauded, Fredrick became angry.

"Shut up all o' you! A man can't think with all this confusion!"

When Zohra suggested that they could use Benje's house for practice, he turned on her.

"Zohra! Stop tellin' me what to do."

Zohra's joy shrivelled up. She retired under the calabash tree.

"It ain't a bit like Christmas," she complained to Veronica. "Fredrick not happy."

The rain poured down relentlessly on Christmas Eve Day. Zohra was not allowed to play outside, so she played by the Christmas tree, looking at the crepe paper to remember Christmas every time she became unhappy. Far away, Fredrick's drum rivalled the thunder.

"You think Santa will come, Mommy?" Zohra asked anxiously.

"He always come."

"Is very special this year, you know."

"Why?"

"I got some letters for him."

"You better give them to me."

"I want to put them under the Christmas tree tonight."

"O.K. then, don't forget."

She wandered about the house pressing her face against the window panes. Rain on the glass distorted everything. The Corentyne River shuddered. Kalamadin's house across the road stretched like plastic to the sky. The world outside looked like reflections distorted in a hall of mirrors. She turned inward to Capa's house and the Christmas tree for security of the familiar.

"You sure the rain won't stop Santa comin'?" Zohra asked again.

"No. He can see through snowstorm at the North Pole, so I'm sure he can come through rain."

"But snow look soft and white in Christmas cards, Mommy," she said anxiously. "He ain't used to rain that fall like needles from our sky."

"Rain like needles?" asked her mother wonderingly.

"Yes, it feel like needles sometimes when I get caught in it."

About three o'clock that day the rain stopped and Zohra ran over to see how Fredrick was getting on. She suggested no improvements that day. Fredrick looked like a rain cloud. He concentrated fiercely on his group and ignored the children. Rain seemed to have washed away the joy and vitality of the previous performances. Nobody smiled. Zohra wandered back home. Madeen was spreading sawdust over the mud in the backyard. He stopped when he saw her.

"You write that letter?" he enquired.

"Yes."

"If that train set don't come, it prove Santa Claus dead."

"He never die. He live forever."

Madeen laughed scornfully.

"We will see," he said, his voice threatening all her beliefs. Then he turned away from her and began sprinkling sawdust again all over the back yard. Zohra went upstairs. Two rejections in one afternoon proved rather depressing. As she levered herself up the stairs, two at a time, she wondered why people seemed so unhappy. When she reached the kitchen at the top of the stairs, the smell of Demerara rum cake and patties dispelled some of her sadness. She sat on the trunk and stared at her familiar friend, the stove.

"What wrong?" asked Gramma.

"It ain't like Christmas."

"Well, tell me why we bakin' so much?"

Her aunt, who had put the last baking tin of cake mixture in the oven, stood looking at Zohra.

"Why you so quiet today?"

Zohra shrugged. Her aunt held out the bowl where she had mixed the ingredients for the cake. "Have a lick of the bowl and the spoon," she said to Zohra.

The child brightened up. She took the bowl on her lap and scraped it clean with the wooden spoon. Her eyes began to shine again. She felt she had tasted some of the ingredients of Christmas.

That evening, dressed in their best nightclothes, Zohra, her brother and cousins took a last look at the Christmas tree before they went to bed. Zohra placed her letters in the jardinière which held the Christmas tree. Then they all went to bed.

Zohra fell into a restless sleep and woke up with a start. She leapt out of bed and ran into the sitting room. The green crepe paper Christmas tree had been transformed. Great baubles hung from its limbs. Zohra examined them. The sitting room contracted and expanded within them. Tinsel twined round the tree like glistening lianas. The child could hardly open her eyes wide enough to encompass all this splendour. She hardly noticed her family watching in amusement.

"Santa Claus!" she cried, seeing her hero of Christmas beaming from the wall beside the Christmas tree.

"I been very good," she said, expecting her oracle to speak. It remained silent.

"Is only a mask, chile," Gramma said.

"Oh, you mean like the ones Fredrick and Big Boy wear for masquerade?" she said, a bit disappointed.

"Yes."

"I thought it was Santa."

"Santa been," her mother said. "Look under the tree there."

Zohra looked. Under the tree, next door to the rocking chair, was a pram.

"Now I really know Santa livin'. Wait till I tell Madeen!" shouted Zohra and stretched out a trembling hand to touch the pram. She ran her fingers over the shiny sides and sniffed the plastic hood.

"Look inside," her uncle said.

A beautiful doll lay there. As Zohra took her out, the blue eyes roused a sound in Zohra's head.

"Sophie," she whispered, then she shouted to her family. "I callin' her Sophie!"

They laughed and the noise woke the other children who came out heavy-eyed from sleep and were awakened by the dazzle of the Christmas tree. They began to find their presents and Zohra took this opportunity to peep into the jardinière. The letters had gone.

"I want to see Madeen face when I show him them presents," she said, and began looking for presents for her friends.

"Where the presents for Sophie and Henry?" she asked her mother.

"Well," said her mother. "Santa didn't have enough place in his bag this year."

"But he bring the pram."

"Yes. You ask for it long ago."

"Madeen countin' on Santa bringin' him train set."

"Madeen has to wait."

"But he will say there ain't a Santa Claus."

"He can have lemonade and cake."

"But he want toys. What about Sophie and Henry?"

"Well, Sophie can have a bottle o' ginger beer and Henry can have patties."

"But they ain't presents."

"Maybe next year Santa will bring them somethin'."

Zohra felt sad. Her friends had no presents. Santa's bag was reputed to be bottomless. They said presents gushed out from it like water from the huge vat in the backyard. She puzzled over the paradox of Christmas when she had presents and her friends did not. She placed Sophie in the pram and pushed her towards the dolls' house near the window.

"At least sun shining," she thought. "Fredrick will have a good day for masqueradin'"

Later that morning, Zohra visited Sophie and Henry. Sophie had just returned from church. She smelt of Ricketts' Crown Blue and Evening in Paris perfume. Her white dress fell snowy against her ebony skin. Sophie's mother snored quietly in a corner of their small room.

"Happy Christmas, Sophie," Zohra said.

"Lawd bless you, chile."

"Sophie, Santa didn't bring anythin' for you," Zohra said slowly, "but Aunty send you a bottle of ginger beer."

"Say thanks fo' me. An' now why you got a long face?"

"I can't understand why I got present and you didn't get any."

"Well, life strange sometimes," Sophie said smiling. "But I got ginger beer from yo' family. That is a present."

"I don't understand."

"Well, while you thinkin' 'bout it, have a glass o' sorrel."

"Not now. I goin' to see Henry."

Sophie let her go and she ran off to see Henry. He sat outside his door smoking. The thin trickle of smoke was the only living thing about him. He wore his old khaki clothes.

"Henry," Zohra said. "Happy Christmas. But why you ain't dress up?"

"I got to clean Metro for two o'clock matinee."

"Me wear a new dress."

"It nice," Henry smiled.

"Henry….."
"What?"
"Santa didn't bring anythin' for you."
"You expect him to?"
"Yes, yes. I write specially. Besides you been very good."
"Well, don't worry 'bout it."
"I got some patties for you, though."

She handed him the parcel which she had wrapped up for him.

"Is a nice present. I will eat it for me dinner."

"It ain't fair, man," cried Zohra. "You did plait me hair when it loose. You even help cut the Christmas tree. You been so nice. It ain't like you are Madeen. He ain't good."

"I think the patties is a nice present," Henry insisted.

Bur Zohra screwed up her face trying to work it all out. She was returning home when she saw Fredrick and his band dancing out of Long Range Yard. Zohra ran upstairs for the money she had saved. When she came down, she saw the Mother Sally looming as tall as the telegraph posts. The children, cinema goers and other villagers crowded in front of Long Range Yard to watch. Mother Sally towered above the band, guarding them. The masks leered grotesquely at the watchers. Zohra only recognised Fredrick because he had his drum. Fenton, dressed as a woman, looked like a badly made up Geisha girl. They all looked like creatures from a nightmare. Yet to Zohra they were the spirit of Christmas. She and the other children danced to the familiar music. Zohra jingled the money in her pocket and shouted at the top of her voice. "Come on, Fredrick! Come on!"

That moment marked the climax of her Christmas feeling. She forgot the strange masks and her earlier disappointment about the presents in an ecstasy of rhythm. As she swirled round, she felt herself united with the drumbeat. The drum stopped. A disharmony of shouts shattered her dance. She looked. Another band of masqueraders had appeared on the road and confronted Fredrick's band

"Big Boy!" people cried.

Zohra shivered in the sunshine as a man in a red mask stalked up to Fredrick.

"I did warn you, Fredrick!" Big Boy roared.

"I got a licence!" yelled Fredrick.

The colossal red mask collided with Fredrick's.

"What happen? People shouldn't fight on Christmas Day," Zohra thought.

The fighters howled. People backed away. Only Sophie rushed forward.

"Keep back, Sophie!" shouted Ismay.

But Sophie hurled herself at Big Boy, hitting him on his arm.

"Stop this brawlin'. This is the birthday of the Lawd, not the devil!" she cried.

"Run for Constable Fernandes," Ismay called to Veronica.

"They gonna murder each other," someone said.

Sophie was pushed back, blood dripping down the front of her white frock. She look dazed. Zohra stood hypnotised by the sweating bodies in the masks and the blood on Sophie's dress. The word 'devil', the heat and the masks conjured up hell in her mind.

"Man, they look live devils, but today is Christmas Day", Zohra thought.

With a cry that no one heard, Zohra ran towards Metro. The paradox between the idea and reality of Christmas had confused her. The joy of masqueraders and crepe paper faded. Zohra only saw the masks. They had deceived her. They projected the hate of Big Boy and Fredrick. Even the Santa Claus mask by the Christmas tree had deceived her, but Zohra did not realise it hid unfairness to the poor like Henry and Sophie. Santa only smiled for those who could afford him. The masks flickered in her mind like primeval nightmares.

She stumbled towards Metro and the refuge of the giant carrion-crow bushes.

"It can't be Christmas," she murmured, looking up for light at the bulbous candles of the carrion-crow bush.

As she lay there, the money she had saved for Fredrick's band rolled out of her pocket. Its dull jingle reminded her that it was still Christmas.

9. Cheat

Zohra had been at primary school for over a year. Miss 'Gusta's school seemed so tiny in comparison with the new school. When she returned to school that September, they had let her skip Big Infants and go up to first standard. She was the youngest in the class.

In first standard, girlish friendships sprang up like razor grass along the trenches: absent yesterday, present today. Maharajin sprouted tall and arrowheaded in the classroom, towering above the other children.

"Bald-head Maharajin!" the boys in her class would shout whenever they saw her. "What you do with your hair, gal? It gone for a walk?"

The thin girl would wince. Yet next day she came to school with more coconut oil on her head. This oil had attracted Zohra long before the jeers. One day after the boys had finished teasing her, Zohra spoke:

"Why you don't put lil' bit oil on you head? It won't look so funny then."

A smile split Maharajin's face, dividing it in two sectors. Her large teeth flowered forth.

"Ma think plenty coconut oil does make hair grow."

"Me don't put any on me head, but it growin'"

Zohra shook her lengthy coils of hair, and Maharajin's eyes glinted like marbles. She pressed the slate to her chest, inclined her head and whispered importantly:

"Typhoid!"

"What?"

"You never hear 'bout it?"

The living marbles bounced heavenwards causing Zohra to feel small and ignorant.

"Well, maybe when you big like me, you will lucky enough to get it."

"What it is?"

"Is special. You only get it when you grow older. Sometimes you sick and dream all sorta nice thing, then you hair drop out."

"It sound horrible."

"But then me dream me eatin' fowl curry and me don't have to fetch water or mind baby."

As Zohra's experience of illness was limited to measles, she never questioned Maharajin's explanation of typhoid. So next time Razack teased her, Zohra related how she had lost her hair.

"Bet you they pull off she hair like paddy plant in rice field!" roared Razack. "Me baby cousin get typhoid, so isn't growin'-up sickness."

"Why you let Maharajin fool you so? Why you so clever at school work and stupid enough to believe she?" Carl asked.

"O.K. You see if me will help you in dictation if you trouble she," Zohra said.

"Why you like she? Man, she so long," said Carl, extending his arms above his head. "Me hate the way she watch people just like cannie-crow."

"But you all tease she all the time. She frighten'," Zohra protested. "Why you don't talk to her?"

"Me would gie 'way all me bunga seeds than come near that oily head," Razack cried.

"Awright, me ain't helpin' you with spelling'," Zohra grumbled when she realised she could not enlist their help.

The boys willingly sacrificed Zohra's help to tease and incite others to torment Maharajin. Zohra felt bound to keep her promise, but she missed the boys. Maharajin's resources seemed limitless. She had an unusual stock of experiences which she readily produced to impress Zohra. Horrified by Zohra's ignorance about the facts of life, she bombarded her reluctant listener with fantastic explanations.

"If you don't know 'bout babies, you must know 'bout keeping wake at funeral?"

"No. But me don't want to hear."

"Well, we all sit round the dead man and sing and beat drum. Is like he gettin' married again. Is good fun. We get puri and nice thing to eat."

"Poor dead man."

"He lucky. He ain't go to worry 'bout this world. He can turn into cat or dog or king in the next life."

"Me wouldn't come. Mommy say me mustn't stay up late in case me late for school next day."

"Ma don't say nothing."

"If me come to school late, me will miss the lesson and fail exam. Then how I goin' to get story book?"

"Story book?"

"Yes, if me do good in exam, Mommy give me story book."

Maharajin fastened her eyes enviously on Zohra.

"What place you come last term?" Zohra asked.

"Me was sick."

"You didn't get report?"

"Teacher Dot write letter to Pa."

"What it say?"

"Pa can't read."

"You coulda bring it home to us. Mommy read."

"You get story book every time you pass exam?"

"Yes."

"As you got plenty, lend me one with picture."

Next day when Zohra brought some books, Maharajin inhaled the smell of their newness greedily.

"Hmm, it smell so good, man. Bring some more for me."

Zohra brought her more books, but Maharajin never returned them,

"Please bring back them book, Maharajin; Mommy asking where they gone."

"Awright, tomorrow."

Her wide smile would have accommodated Zohra and all her books. Yet tomorrow never came for Maharajin. Each day they met, she asked about the books and Maharajin earnestly promised to bring them. Carl Thomas heard Zohra asking Maharajin to return the books on one occasion.

"She thief you books, silly-billly," he said. "Or maybe she father pawn them fo' buy rum. Mother say they not fit fo' good people to live near."

"But she forget, Carl."

Carl only laughed and went to tell the other boys about it. Next day they began to call Maharajin 'Thiefman'.

The end of the term drew near and Zohra became preoccupied with exams. She forgot about the books and noticed that Maharajin had not come for the exams. However, she came the next Monday.

"Where you been?" Zohra asked.

"Me get fever."

"Well, Miss Dottie sick two day last week, so we have to do some exam this week. You can make some marks still."

Maharajin opened her mouth and blinked her marbles.

"They ain't finish?"

"No. We got Mental Arithmetic this mornin'. Me hate it. You lucky not to wear shoes."

"Why?"

"I can't count right if me got plenty sums to count. I only got ten finger and me toes hiding in shoes."

Zohra became engrossed in the torture of wearing shoes that she never noticed Maharajin's eyes lingering hungrily over them. The school bell rang and they went in dismally to Mental Arithmetic.

Afterwards, Zohra and the boys forgot their disagreement as they stood by the door working out how many questions they had answered correctly. Maharajin lingered by the blackboard watching them.

"Number twenty was ten yam," Kofi said. "Number two was seven chair."

"I got thirteen outa twenty," shouted Carl. "What you get, Zohra?"

"Nineteen. Is the first time me do so good. But Maharajin help me. She lend she toes to count."

She nodded gratefully to the spidery figure in the background.

"Tell me what you get," she coaxed Maharajin.

But Maharajin, lacking the support of her slate which had joined others in a pile to be marked, embraced her shift-clad body, shut her eyes and remained silent.

"Thiefman know better," Kofi cried. "We ain't stupid like Zohra. We all know you thief she story book. Ain't that why you frighten to come near we?"

"Stop it, Kofi. She only forget them," Zohra said. "Come talk to we," she urged Maharajin.

But the boys just guffawed and ran outside to play.

"They won't trouble you if you play with them," Zohra said sadly after they had gone.

"Them man is chamar," cried Maharajin, spitting on the doorpost.

"Miss Dottie will vex if she see you," said Zohra sitting on the steps.

Maharajin looked at Zohra curiously. A long, hungry lizard might have gazed at an unsuspecting fly flitting before it in the same way.

"You ain't glad to get nineteen outa twenty?"

"Yes, thanks for you toes. Is a pity though."

"What?"

"Only one mo' mark to get twenty outa twenty."

Maharajin's eyes crept towards the slates. They stood piled up on the edge of the classroom bench.

"Is easy."

"What?"

"Look fo' you slate and change the answer."

"That's cheatin'."

"Man, you want twenty outa twenty, not me."

"Teacher Dottie will vex."

"She won't know. Nobody here but us."

"It ain't right."

"O.K. me will mind me own business. I ain't want nothing', is you."

Maharajin turned her back on Zohra, who felt very uneasy. She stared at her shoes, the slats in the school wall, then at the empty classroom. Somehow the place seemed so vast after the children had left, and the pile of slates so small. To correct one error on a tiny slate in that huge space suddenly seemed an unimportant wrong.

"One mark ain't plenty. Nobody else will get nineteen outa twenty," Zohra thought. "Who will know?"

"You comin' to buy sugar cake?"

"Mommy will be so glad if I get all them sums right."

"You comin'?"

"Is so easy. I only got to change three to eight."

"Let we go out, Zohra."

Zohra sat clenching her fists and biting her lip in an agony of indecision. Maharajin had turned round to look at her.

"It quick and easy, Zohra. Nobody here. Take the slate pencil."

Zohra was only half-aware that she snatched the pencil, flew over to the stack of slates and began to look at the name on each slate. Gradually, she turned from the front of the classroom where Maharajin hovered like a discoloured gawling, craning her neck towards the door. Zohra gently nudged the tops of the slates till she came to hers. She gasped with relief.

"Zohra, what you doing there?"

The long slate pencil fell to the floor with a harsh crack. Zohra faced round, the noise of the pencil still in her ears.

"Miss," the word fell hissing on the air. "She cheatin', so me call you."

"I 'shamed o' you. How many times we all write on the blackboard 'Honesty is the best policy'?" Miss Dot said severely.

Zohra shivered, only aware of the figure at her teacher's side.

"You givin' she nought fo' cheatin', nah Miss?" Maharajin asked.

"Quiet Maharajin, go sit down now," Teacher Dot said. "Bring you slate, Zohra."

Mechanically, Zohra brought her slate. Meanwhile Maharajin sat like an audience of one at a play, her glassy eyes absorbing the mirroring the scene of woe. The teacher took Zohra's slate and looked at it.

"Since when you get nineteen outa twenty in Mental Arithmetic? Look like you been cheating."

Deliberately, and with a great sense of ceremony, Teacher Dot drew a gigantic nought on the slate. Zohra felt her soul dwindle into nothingness.

"Stand in front of that blackboard till class come in. Hold up you slate."

Zohra stood, head down.

"Order! Order, Standard 1!" commanded Miss Dot. "Stop that giggling, Veronica! O.K. Listen. Something bad happen during recreation period."

Teacher Dot's tone became so severe that the classroom sounds stopped.

"Zohra didn't obey the class motto. What it is?"

The class was well indoctrinated.

"Honesty is the best policy."

"She cheat. Maharajin saw her and tell me."

Here, undertones of 'Baldie' and 'Thiefman' came from the boys' section.

"Quiet!"

Teacher Dot took the chalk from her table and wrote 'Cheat' on Zohra's slate.

Zohra began to cry and again voices rose in the class.

"Open your mouth again, and mark me, you going to join Zohra here," threatened Miss Dottie.

No one spoke.

"Get the swibble-jack."

The classroom may well have become the cemetery outside, for a similar hush fell on the children.

"Carl Thomas, get the swibble-jack from Mr. Ramlall."

The swibble-jack was a twig used only as a punishment for grave offences. It stung sharply for hours after use. Reluctantly, Carl brought the swibble-jack. Miss Dot administered the punishment before the whole class.

Afterwards, Zohra stood before the class holding her slate. The afternoon tottered on as Zohra's tears fell on the slate and gradually dried there. Maharajin sat on, gorging herself on this spectacle, oblivious of everything else.

10. The Move

One day, Zohra returned home to find Gramma's chicken coop empty.

"What happen to your fowls, Gramma?" she asked when she reached the kitchen.

"I sell them,"

"But why? You always so proud of your Rhode Island fowls."

"There ain't goin' to be place in the new house."

"New house?"

"Yes. We leavin' Capa house."

"Leavin' Capa house?"

Zohra sat down on the trunk slowly. It seemed impossible to disassociate herself with this familiar kitchen. The stove still gorged wood as it had done when Miss Omega visited and the fire in the fireside continued to remind her of Mrs. Kalamadin.

"But Gramma, we mustn't go."

"Why?"

"'Cause Capa house….."

Zohra threw her arms open to express how much she loved the place. Yet how could she explain in words? She could not say that the house grew like a dark fruit ripening with ideas which flowered for her. From its secret corners a mystery projected outward into the backyard by the vat, extending to Long Range and along the brick path to Metro. Capa's house had always been the centre of her universe. Zohra felt an inner chaos which she could not communicate to Gramma when she thought of the move.

"Is not the same anywhere else," she said at last.

"Nowhere is the same, chile," Gramma said. "Is a hard lesson to learn. Drink you milk."

Zohra felt too sick to drink the milk. She left it on the table and went to sit on the back steps. Grip yapped as he chased a lizard in the back yard. She could hear Ismay scolding Veronica. Nearby, the electricity generator throbbed in time to the painful rhythm of her heart. Inside the kitchen she heard her mother come in and ask Gramma, "Where Zohra?"

"On the steps."

"You tell her?"

"Yes. I tell her 'bout movin'."

Zohra crept downstairs miserably and walked down Metro path.

"I ain't goin'," Zohra decided. "I stayin' here."

She went to see Henry; he was opening the shutters of the cinema for the four o'clock matinee.

"Henry, we movin' to a new house."

"What?"

"We leavin' Metro Yard."

He carefully opened the shutters, then turned round.

"Where you goin'?"

"I don't know."

He felt for his cigarettes in his breast pocket. He took one out and tapped it against the matchbox.

"When you goin'?"

"I don't know."

"Don't forget to come an' say goodbye."

Zohra nodded and ran away from Henry for the first time in her life. Outside the sun made the tears rainbow coloured in her eyes. She forced them back and marched home again.

That night Zohra talked to Gramma about the move.

"Why I can't stay here with Uncle Mus?"

"He already got his own chil'ren."

"But I can't go away from Capa house and Sophie and Henry."

"You all can see one another sometimes."

"Who I will play with?"

"You can play with Nizam."

"He always breakin' me things."

"Because he small. He will grow up and you will like the new house."

"No, I will hate it."

"It got water toilet and light bulbs."

Zohra shook her head stubbornly,

"When we movin'?"

"Next week."

That night Zohra dreamt of the new house. Its windows peered at her wherever she went. The doors laughed, blowing her inward. Suddenly, she heard a sucking noise. The doors and windows of the new house began sucking in Capa's house, Metro and Long Range. They became smaller and smaller until they disappeared. Zohra hammered against the new white walls to let them out again.

When she woke up, the morning sun streamed in belittling the horror of her dream. But by the time she had dressed, she knew the only way to save Capa's house was to stay in it.

When the family began to pack a few days later, her mother said, "You want to see the new house?"

"No," Zohra said.

"It lovely. You can walk from the backyard right to the beach. And there ain't no bats there."

Bats lived in the eaves of Capa's house and accidentally found their way inside sometimes.

"No."

Nizam went to visit the house with the other members of the family. He returned full of excitement.

"I flush the toilet five times,"

Zohra bent closer over her reading book.

"You listenin'? I switch on the lights and been to the beach with Mommy."

"You can't see I readin'?" she snapped at him.

Everyone became busier as the time for the move approached. The bedroom and the sitting room grew barer. Zohra grew quieter.

"Where your red dress, Zohra?" asked her mother the day before the move.

"I don't know."

"I see it yesterday. And look under the bed for your black shoes."

Zohra looked, but neither of these were found. On the morning of the move, neighbours came to say goodbye, as the truck was loaded. No one missed Zohra until the truck was about to leave.

"Where Zohra?" asked her mother.

"Amin, call Zohra," said Uncle Mus.

"She ain't there," said Amin.

"That chile always gettin' into mischief," grumbled her mother coming upstairs.

Everyone searched for her while the truck waited. In the end, Gramma sent off the rest of the family and stayed behind to look for her.

"Madeen, go ask Sophie and Henry if they see her," Gramma said.

Madeen ran off on this errand.

"Is just like the time she hide before," Gramma said to her son, Mus. "She been very quiet these last few days."

"She will come back," Mus said. "Is a good thing all the chil'ren not so mischievous."

Gramma nodded, but she looked worried.

"Zohra! Zohra!" she called as she went upstairs. "Come here, chile!"

Gramma's voice floated out of the house to the fowl coop where Zohra hid. She clutched a small carton box bulging with clothes which she had smuggled out of the house. Though Gramma had cleaned the coop, it smelt of chickens. Zohra held her nose and breathed through her mouth for a bit. Through the chicken mesh, she saw Madeen stalking round the vat. His green eyes narrowed as he bent to peep under the vat. Zohra stopped breathing through her mouth and lay still. Madeen straightened up shaking his head.

"Hey Zohra! Zohra where you deh, girl?" he cried.

Zohra did not move. She watched hypnotised as his long legs approached the chicken coop. For the first time she noticed how the hair on his legs gleamed like golden fur in the sunlight.

"Me know you there," he said.

But as Zohra did not move, the golden legs walked past slowly towards the generator house. A few minutes later, she heard him prodding the zinc walls of the generator house with a stick. The sound ceased abruptly, there was a rustle of bushes and then silence. She eased her left leg forward and changed position slightly. The sun grew warmer through the tin roof. Zohra became drowsy.

When she awoke, the heat had died. Dew glistened on buck bead bushes nearby. The distant footsteps of cinema goers pounded on the brick path to Metro.

"Must be people goin' to five o'clock matinee," Zohra thought. She rubbed her eyes and peeped through the wire mesh. Beyond the vat, she could see the empty backyard. Hunger, coupled with the growing stench of the coop drove her from this hiding place. Zohra scrambled out clutching the carton box. Quietly, she ran past the generator house hiding in the bushes till no one was about. Then the child ran across to Metro, hid by the cinema steps, then crept round the back towards Henry's room. Once she reached it, Zohra looked for him, but no one was there.

Zohra sat on the stool and looked at the old cinema posters which Henry had used to brighten his drab walls. The Three Musketeers lunged at her with their swords. Characters from "Ship Ahoy" danced along the wall and flames poured out of Scarlet O'Hara's house from a poster of "Gone With The Wind". Now Zohra could read, she climbed on to the table and began reading the posters. When Henry returned, he found her kneeling on the table trying to read in the darkening room.

"Zohra, what you doin' here?" he demanded.
"Just readin'."
"Everybody lookin' for you."
"I ain't goin' to the new house."
"You got to."
"No, Henry. I come to live with you."
Henry lit a cigarette.
"Come down, Zohra," he said quietly.
Instead, she sat on the table dangling her legs.
"Look, I bring me clothes," she said, pointing to the battered carton box.
"Where you been?"
"Hidin'."
"You mess up your dress. Wait till your mother catch you."
"She won't. I livin' with you now."
"But you can't."
"Why?"
Henry inhaled his cigarette smoke deeply, then exhaled it.
"They is your family. You belong to them."

"But I want to change 'cause I don't want to leave Capa house and you and Sophie. So why I can't be your family?"

"You can't change your family."

"But Grip belong to Fredrick mother before he live with us. Now he live with us. Why I can't change?"

"Chil'ren and dogs is two different things."

"Why? I always want to live with you and sweep Metro and see pictures."

"You can't, Zohra," said Henry. "What your family will think? Besides, I ain't got enough money."

But money meant little to Zohra.

"You don't like me, Henry?"

"Yes. Yes." He said.

"Then why I can't stay with you?"

"Zohra," Henry tried again. "If I let you stay, they will think I steal you. Then police will lock me up."

"But I will tell the police I come specially to live with you."

"You got to go!" Henry said at last.

Zohra gripped the edge of the small table and twined her legs round the table legs, bracing herself for a struggle.

"No," she said.

Henry only looked at her. She felt just as she did when the pigeons died. Her stomach felt tight and her head was dizzy.

"I will go if you don't like me," Zohra said, challenging him to deny it, yet terrified he would.

Henry gently rolled his lighted cigarette between his fingers. Zohra watched fascinated as the thin curl of smoke stayed in the same place.

"You know it very hard, Zohra," Henry said at last.

"What hard?"

"That you leavin' Metro Yard."

"Then you will let me stay?" she cried hopefully.

"No."

Zohra sank back sadly on the table. Henry's voice sounded strange as though he had slammed his fingers in the shutters of the cinema.

"You O.K.?" she asked when he did not speak.

He just bowed his head.

She leapt off the table and knelt by him.

"You not havin' a stroke?"

He shook his head.

"Then what wrong?"

"You got to take your clothes back now."

The nightmare of the new house sucking in everything reappeared in her mind. She shivered. "But everythin' will disappear."

"What?"

"Oh Henry!" she cried, grabbing hold of his free hand. "I afraid of the new house."

He let his cigarette drop to the floor and stamped it out.

"You don't like me?" she asked. "You ain't my friend?"

Tears pricked her eyes, but she refused to cry. She just hugged herself to keep off the cold of the nightmare.

"There ain't no use cryin'," Henry said.

"I ain't cryin' even though you don't like me."

"Zohra," Henry said with a great effort as though he was lifting a huge stack of cinema seats. "Me like you…..me like you mo' than anybody else."

"What?"

"You hear me first time."

"Then how you can send me away?"

"Because me like you."

"I don't understand."

"Look Zohra, how I can afford to give you nice clothes, house or food?"

"I got enough clothes and if I'm near Capa house, is O.K."

"We talk enough, come on," he said getting up and picking up the box. He tried to take her hand, but she backed away against the wall, dwarfed by the figures of the Three Musketeers.

"Listen to this story, Zohra," Henry said, sitting down again. He put down the box and said, "Come here."

Zohra came towards him hesitantly. Gently, he took her on his knee as he had done a long time ago when she had bruised her knee.

"Listen. Long time ago in Essequibo, me used to live with Ma an' Pa. I was the youngest in the family. Ma an' Pa very ole. A snake bite Pa and he die. Then Ma went to live with me big brother Harold. He didn't want me. One day, he beat me so bad that I run away from his house. That's when I begin cleaning cinema. When I get a little bigger, they give me watchman work too. So for years I doin' this work, chile. An' it look like I will die sweepin' cinema."

"Your brother did beat you bad, Henry?" Zohra asked.

"Yes, look" he said, making her get down from his knee. Then he took off his shirt and showed her the marks on his back.

"Poor Henry," said Zohra, touching the lowest mark. "You right to run away."

"Maybe, but I run away because nobody love me. Now you runnin' away from your family who love you. You don't like your Gramma an' Mommy an' everybody?"

"Yes, but I scared to leave here."

"Why?"

"Capa house and you and Sophie won't be there."

"We will come to see you. We can come and see the house."

"You think so?"

"Yes. Runnin' away don't help anythin', Zohra. They will find you tomorrow or the next day."

"Your brother find you?"

"Yes, and he give me more licks."

"You think they will beat me?"

"I don't think so, if you go back now."

"And you sure I can't live with you?"

"No, Zohra. If you born with one set of people, you stay with them till you grow up."

"Henry, I can sleep here tonight?"

"No, Zohra. They worried."

He looked down at her and gently tugged a lock of hair.

"You loss your hair ribbon," he said.

"You takin' me back?"

He nodded, then bent down to her level.

"I takin' you back because is the best thing."

"And you still like me?"

Henry nodded, then lifted her off the floor into his arms. He smelt of cigarettes and Brylcream. He moved out of the room into the yard. His gentleness silenced Zohra who quietly enjoyed the comfort and motion of being carried. They crunched up Metro path till they came to Capa's house. Grip began to bark. As Henry went to the back steps, Gramma, Uncle Mus and her mother came to the door.

"I just find her," Henry said.

"Thank God, Henry!" her mother said.

"Where you been?" Gramma said.

Henry placed Zohra in the centre of the kitchen and looked down at her. "She come to say goodbye," Henry said. "Behave good, Zohra. I will come to see you."

"But Henry….." Zohra cried.

He smiled, waved at her and went through the black cavity of the kitchen door into the night. Zohra felt she had lost him forever. She began to cry.

"What happen? Where you been all this time?" her mother asked.

Her family walled her in with their concern. Zohra felt bewildered.

"You too big to run away," Uncle Mus said. "Man, you make us so worried."

"Why you run away, chile?" Gramma asked.

"I don't want to leave Capa house or Henry or Sophie", Zohra said.

"You mean you love them more than us?" her mother demanded.

Zohra could not reply. Since she had talked to Henry, she had become unsure whether she loved the house and her neighbours or her family. Until the move, all three were fused together. Now the division confused her.

"When last you eat?" Gramma asked, breaking the tension.

Zohra wiped away the tears with her knuckles and glad of an escape from her mother's question, replied "This mornin'."

"Ma, let her answer me," her mother persisted. "You spoilin' her, you know."

"After she eat," Gramma said. "Now why you all don't go and find somethin' else to do."

Zohra's mother sighed.

"At least she safe," she said.

"Yes," Gramma said. "It could ha' been worse."

"Well, I better get back to the shop or Madeen will eat all the bulls' eyes," said Uncle Mus, and he went downstairs again.

"Go lie down," Gramma said to Zohra's mother. "You work hard today."

Soon her mother went upstairs and they were alone.

"What really wrong, Zohra?" Gramma asked, sitting down before her at the kitchen table. In the yellow lamplight, her hair looked grey. As Zohra ate, her eyes followed the wrinkles which channelled Gramma's mouth and eyes. She looked old.

"You distress me a lot, Zohra," Gramma said. "I think you really gone this time."

"Me sorry," Zohra said.

"Why you go?"

"Me love Capa house."

"And you think I don't love it, chile? I love every floorboard in this house. Was the first house your Capa an' I got. How we struggle hard to save an' buy it. Your grandfather was a hard-workin' man, and he make me work hard too, but it worth while, chile. I live here fifty years. I had me chil'ren here, I see Capa die here. I thought I would die here too, but it ain't God's will. Is a big grief to leave here."

"I didn't know, Gramma."

"Now you gettin' big, you must behave. Was a shock when you disappear. I really frighten, man."

"You too frighten, Gramma?"

"You think people get too ole to frighten? No, chile. Every time one fear go, another one come."

"Henry say you can't leave the people you born with, you got to stay with them."

"Henry right. You think this house will be the same if we leave? When we and all the furniture gone, it will be different. We make it live."

Zohra thought as she swallowed her food slowly. "If I stay here, maybe Henry could come to live with me."

"Even if Henry come," Gramma smiled and her wrinkles melted away. "It won't be the same. The house nice because we all live here and make it happy. But we can't always have what we want. How much time I tell meself that. Yet no kitchen can be like this kitchen."

Zohra's eyes followed Gramma around the huge kitchen as she walked round, touching objects tenderly. And as Zohra shared the feeling of loss with Gramma, she felt that with Gramma as an ally, the new house need not be so frightening.

11. Ole Man

Zohra became slowly reconciled to the new house. The splintered light from the Muranese glass windows at the front of the house translated her too abruptly into a new world. So she spent much time looking at the river and Ole Man's house from the kitchen window.

Ole Man was a fisherman who took care of the backyard after his work had finished for the day. He often sat on his verandah enmeshed in seines as he mended them.

"Ole Man always so quiet," she thought. "All he do is smoke cigarettes and look at people."

At nightfall, after a long day's fishing, he would play the sitar. The sound rose discordantly, splintering her mind like the light of the Muranese glass windows. Yet it throbbed like wind and had the softness of the river. On the moonlight nights, she liked to watch Ole Man and the other fishermen hauling home their catch of gallibaca or snook. Then the fish lay on the verandah enmeshed in silver scales.

One day as she drew water from the standpipe outside Ole Man's house, he lay in his hammock staring at the shadow of oleander leaves.

"Howdy," he said.

"You catch any fish today?" Zohra enquired.

"Not much."
"Why?"
"Sometimes is like that."
Her bucket overflowed and she turned off the tap.
"Is luck, you know," Ole Man murmured.
"Luck?"
"If you don't have luck, you done for."
"You always catch plenty fish."
"Not always."
"But everybody say you is the best fisherman on the Corentyne."
"One day, one day, gonga te."
"What?"
"Maybe me luck finish."
"But why?"
"Maybe Wata Mama ain't like me no more."
"Wata Mama?"
"She give we fisherman luck."
"Oh."
"If she want, she can curse we so we not get any fish."

Zohra had heard of Old Hags and Jumbees but not Wata Mama. The thought made her nervous.

"Me hope you get some fish."

She picked up her bucket.

"We will see."

After this conversation, Zohra took a keen interest in Ole Man. Every day she would ask, "Ole Man catch any fish?"

"Why you ask?" Gramma said.

"Nothin'."

"That make five time you ask this week,"

"He got any today?"

"Yes, yes. When Ole Man does never get fish?"

Zohra shrugged. She felt Ole Man had entrusted her with a special piece of information, so she said nothing else.

A few weeks later, Zohra went for a walk on the sea wall. The river stretched taut, projecting isolated fishing boats. Something vertical stood on the deck of a red one.

"Is a man or a mast?" Zohra wondered, shading her eyes. Then it moved and threw something in the water.

"Oh, he got on white singlet," she thought. "It must be Ole Man and that must be Sea Lion. He throwin' somethin' in the water."

Impelled by her curiosity, Zohra ran down the sea wall and rushed into the water. She could see Ole Man clearly now.

"His eyes closed. What floatin' on the water?" She strained her eyes.

"Hibiscus and oleander! And he look funny, almost like Benje when we think he got stroke." She stood ankle-deep in water, uncertain whether to interrupt him. Then he opened his eyes and threw something else in the water. It landed noiselessly.

"Red hibiscus!" she whispered.

At this point, Ole Man looked at her. She felt as strangely as she did when Muranese windows shone in moonlight. She began to turn away.

"Where you goin'?" he called.

"Home. Got any fish today?"

"No luck."

"Oh."

"But maybe Wata Mama will hear me."

"Why?"

"I just do pooja."

Zohra remembered the flowers. Hindus always offered flowers as part of the ritual in prayer.

"I do pooja so Wata Mama can help me."

He sounded as though he were talking to himself. Only the gentle breeze and the patient rustle of coconut palms surrounded them.

"If only me luck can born again."
"I goin' home now."
"No, no, wait."

Zohra waited. Ole Man swung from the boat and waded through the scattered offerings. He stopped before the small girl and looked down at her.

"You got luck,"
"Luck?"
"Your luck new born."
"What you mean?"
"Give me you luck."
"But….."
"Wata Mama can't refuse that. Your luck fresh like them hibiscus flower. Give me you luck."

Zohra stared at his pleading face, unsure of his meaning.

"But me can't give you anythin'. Ask Gramma."
"Say you givin' me you luck."

Zohra felt his intensity and urgency. She grew frightened.

"Me goin'!" she cried, and ran out of the water quickly.
"Wait! Wait!"

But the child ran faster until she reached the sea wall. Then for a moment she looked round. Ole Man was just another vertical line in the glass of the river. He no longer looked threatening. Yet she ran on, feeling as though the world had turned to Muranese glass and Ole Man was the biggest splinter of frightening light.

Zohra did not visit the beach for sometime afterwards in case she met Ole Man. Once she tiptoed past him as he sat on his empty fish cart.

"Ole Man got any fish today?" Zohra asked Aunty Jai after she had returned home.

"Thing bad with poor Ole Man. He not been well."

Though Zohra avoided Ole Man physically, she was obsessed by his sad face and strange request. After her evening meal, she would sit quietly behind the kitchen window to listen to his sitar.

"The thing cryin'," she used to think.

Sound splintered her mind like slow-moving spikes of light. Yet she felt compelled to listen. One evening, Ole Man did not play his sitar. The child worried about this.

"What wrong with Ole Man?"

"He ain't feelin' well."

"Poor Ole Man."

"His daughter say is the first time in years he sick."

Zohra felt guilty. After a restless night, she decided to go and see Ole Man. She made an excuse to go into the backyard next morning. "Me will just pass the verandah; me won't look," she promised herself. As she passed Ole Man's verandah, she heard the ropes of his hammock creak and did look. Ole Man lay in his hammock wrapped up in a seine. He seemed asleep.

"His beard growin'," Zohra thought. "And how he rockin' about."

He suddenly woke with a start and looked round wildly. Zohra tried to run away but her limbs froze. He tore at the seine round his body violently. "They catchin' me! They catchin' me!" he cried.

The man's energy was so great that she felt frozen to the spot. She could not look away. He ripped off the seine, leapt out of the hammock and stood panting. At first he seemed to look through Zohra. Again she felt the splinters of light penetrating her. Then his energy ebbed and he saw her.

"Is you," he breathed heavily. "Me just had a bad dream."

Zohra could not answer.

"Me dream Wata Mama catchin' me in seine. Man it so real....."

"You sick?" she asked trembling.

"Me luck gone. Me ain't catch no fish."

"Sorry you sick."

Ole Man waved a tired arm at her.

"Zohra! Zohra!" Gramma called from the kitchen window. "Is nearly school time!"

Zohra seized this summons as an excuse and escaped. Upstairs, Gramma looked at her rather sternly.

"What you disturb Ole Man for? He ain't well."

"Me didn't do nothin'."

"The doctor comin' to see him."

"He sick bad?"

"Yes. But he won't go to hospital."

Now Zohra felt convinced that Ole Man was seriously ill. One went to the dispenser for ordinary illnesses. The hospital meant that Ole Man must be very ill. She worried all day about him. She never saw the sums on the blackboard. Instead, Zohra saw Ole Man wresting the seine from his body. "He did look like a dead man, wrap up like that," she thought, then frightened at the idea of death, she thought, "But he can't die. He is the best fisherman on the Corentyne."

After school that day, she asked Gramma again about him.

"He really sick. Aunty goin' to take down some soup."

"Me want to go."

"Ask your Aunty."

After much persuasion, her aunt agreed that she should come. Ole Man's daughter sat by the hammock wiping the sweat from his face.

"How he deh?" Aunty said.

"Bad. Doctor say he got weak heart. Me wish he would go to hospital," the daughter said.

"Why he ain't goin'?"

Ole man suddenly sat up.

"Me can't go," he said to Aunty. "Tell them not to take me there, Missis."

"But why?"

"Me can't leave the river."

"You ain't realise how bad you sick, Ole Man?"

"Hospital can't help me, only a sign, only….."

He sank back again whispering.

"What he say?" Aunty asked.

The daughter looked frightened.

"Oh Aunty, he say Wata Mama. Me frighten bad. He been talkin' 'bout Wata Mama all the time."

"Don't worry."

"But is almost like he gettin' out his head."

Zohra shuddered.

"Ole Man ain't mad," she said.

"What you know 'bout madness, chile?" Aunty asked.

Zohra could only see Ole Man and his offerings.

"He ain't mad," she said to herself.

Again the world of the Muranese glass windows advanced. She moved away from the verandah and stood under the oleander tree. "Maybe if me could give him me luck," she thought, "then he might get better. Tomorrow I will ask him to take it."

Then she felt less guilty about Ole Man. That night she slept more deeply than she had done for weeks. But a hammering on the back door wakened her. Her aunt ran to see what had happened. Zohra and the family followed. Ole Man's daughter stood in the fading moonlight wringing her hands. Her beautiful black hair swathed her as though in mourning. She was weeping.

"Pa run 'way to sea wall, Aunty. He just jump outa the hammock and run. He say he gone to Sea Lion."

"You call Mr. Ferguson to help?"

"He ain't answerin' the door."

"Wait, I comin'."

Aunty Jai ran to the bedroom, threw on some clothes and shouted to Gramma, "Call Mr. Ferguson and send him down to the beach." Then she disappeared with Ole Man's daughter down the back steps.

"Go back to sleep," Gramma said to Zohra.

"Me can't."

"Well, sit down and wrap up in a blanket."

So Zohra sat in a big Morris chair, smothered in a blanket. She saw Ole Man again; his bloodshot eyes pleaded with her. The child shrank into her blanket. Then she thought she heard the sobbing sitar. But outside her all remained quiet for a time.

First, the weeping broke the stillness. They rushed to the kitchen window. In the waning moonlight they saw Mr. Ferguson carrying Ole Man in his arms. The fisherman's white singlet gleamed through patchworks of mango and oleander leaves. It looked like scales of fish Ole Man himself had once hauled into the yard.

"He dead! He dead!" wailed the daughter.

"Oh me God!" cried Zohra's mother, then remembering the child, she said "Go inside."

Zohra could not move.

"Go on."

But Zohra clung to the window sill, staring at the old fisherman's body.

"What happen?" her mother asked.

"He just lyin' like this on Sea Lion," the daughter sobbed. "His head bleedin' and he holdin' oleander flower."

Zohra began to shiver.

"Go in," her mother urged.

"I can't go in," the child whispered and thought. "He don't need me luck now. Is too late."

A great sadness fell upon her. It surrounded her as completely as the Muranese glass world, cutting into her heart and sobbing wildly like Ole Man's sitar.

12. Reconciliation.

The glass world of grief into which Zohra had retreated quivered as the storm lashed the new house. Thunder travelled across the sky like hordes of rampaging dancers. It was as though a celestial Fredrick had lost control of a universe of mad dancers. They pounded across the arena of the sky. Wind sprayed through chinks in the jalousies spitting viciously at her through the mosquito net. Somewhere above it all, she thought she heard Ole Man's sitar.

The lightning became a dragon outside her window, breathing fire into the holes of the jalousies and ventilation slats by the ceiling. It hissed at her when the thunder stopped. Zohra felt the whole universe had turned against her. She closed her eyes willing it to end. When it did, she fell asleep to the regular drumbeat of rain on the zinc roof.

Next morning her mother's voice woke her.

"It rain bad last night. Coconut tree fall down and window break."

Zohra opened her eyes to find friendly sunlight pouring gold through the jalousies instead of dragon fire. The sounds of people drawing water from the well for the morning chores and the river's lap against the sea wall chased away any remnant of disquiet. She rose and went into the sitting room.

Gramma and her mother were looking at the remains of the Muranese glass window. Sumintra, Ole Man's daughter, who helped in the house, came to sweep it up.

"Mornin' everybody," Zohra said.

"You hear the thunder and lightnin' last night?" her mother asked.

"Yes, me thought the roof would fly away," Zohra said.

"We lucky only window break," Gramma said. "Last night me thought the sea wall would break and the river would flood us out. But the river look calm today."

Zohra ran to the windows at the back of the house. The Corentyne winked in the sunlight. The blue sky arced over it to join in the fun. Its gaiety affected Zohra for the first time since Ole Man's death. She hummed an old tune of Fredrick's as she opened the back door and went to the verandah.

"You will catch cold, chile," her mother called. But she did not hear. The world lay newly washed. Coconut fronds beckoned her down into the backyard. Guava and lime trees glistened as though polished.

"It is so beautiful," Zohra whispered. "Maybe the dancers in the thunder last night break up everythin', then make it new again."

She inhaled the smell of grass and earth fulfilled by rain, then unable to resist the call of all this beauty, ran downstairs shouting "I comin'! I comin'!"

All the feelings of love, beauty and pain she had ever felt in her relationships with people whom she had met brimmed over and merged in a feeling of universal joy.